DESERT BURNING

RICK GREENBERG

D1736108

"Still suffering from PTSD, Vietnam vet Rick Green struggles to keep a job while facing the loss of his marriage and children. After the Marines decide to let him back in the reserves, Green quickly takes advantage of the opportunity and soon acquires both a new job and a new wife. When TV newscasters start reporting on a possible call-up of forces in the Persian Gulf, though, Rick worries this trip to the desert may be his last Ooh Rah. Brimming with love of family, country, and Marine Corps, this poignant tale will appeal to past and present Marines as well as anyone who values honor and duty."

—Angela McRae, Line Editor, Red Adept Editing

"Readers will experience the Gulf War in a whole new way with this intimate personal look through the eyes of a Marine."

—Irene S., Proofreader, Red Adept Editing

DEDICATION

I've dedicated this book to the men and women of the first Gulf War. Each one faced the dangers of death while keeping a proud Marine Corps heritage. Living in the desert for months waiting for a ground war to begin, they stayed the course until called upon to put their lives at risk. The number of casualties we were expected to take was in the thousands. The constant threat of chemical warfare kept us all on high alert. Through it all, they never wavered.

ACKNOWLEDGEMENT

A special thank you to my wife who was there through endless re-writes with constant proof reads. Her help was enormous and the book goes nowhere without her.

Once again I owe so much to the group of fabulous writers I have had the honor to be associated with, The Wannabe Writers of The Villages. They were with me through every step of the way.

To Angela McRae, my Line Editor, Red Adept Editing who worked with me not once, not twice, but through three edits, thank you Angela.

To the wonderful proofreader, Irene S. who went over the book to make sure everything was in order.

To Katherine Schumm, who put together the photos and the cover. Her professional work is unmatched by anyone I know. Thank you Katherine, your work was great, as always.

And finally to the men and women of Engineer Support Company who worked tirelessly in a dangerous and an unforgiving environment. Through it all, they performed and held true to the highest standards of the United States Marine Corps tradition.

CHAPTER 1

A NEW LIFE

24 February 1991

THE MINEFIELD ERUPTS WITH AN explosion forty yards to my right. My A driver, Sergeant Ford, shouts, "What the fuck was that!"

I don't answer because I believe it was enemy artillery. Another explosion to my left confirms my fears. Without thinking, I blurt out, "They've got us bracketed, Ford. The next rounds are going to be dead-on!"

His lips tremble as he cries out, "What the hell are you talking about?"

I try to remain calm even though I know this might be the end. "We're bracketed. As soon as those guns get confirmation, they'll rain down on us. Remember the Iraqi ambush the captain warned us about? We're in it."

"We gotta get out of here! Do something!"

"Do what, Ford? We're trapped."

He looks left and right then behind, and I see his fears take root. I try to calm the sergeant, telling him, "There's nowhere to go. Cool down. We'll be okay."

Ford pays no attention. He's scared. I get that. But when he shouts that he's getting out, I yell, "Stay where you are, Sergeant! That's an order!" I take a deep breath and say, "Think what you're doing. You want to tell those drivers Iraqi artillery is about to come down on them? Tell them they have two minutes to get their MOPP suits on? To get out of their trucks? What's going to happen?"

Ford stops, looks at the convoy, and says, "Not good."

"Yeah, man, not good." I give it a moment. "We order them to start evacuating their vehicles, they might panic. Guys might end up in those minefields. And where should I send them? Forward? To the rear? What if they're caught in the open? Where will those shells land? It's best to stay in our trucks and ride it out."

Ford seems to accept our situation as he calms down and stares out the front window. "How many vehicles you figure are out here, Staff Sergeant?"

"Don't know. Could be a thousand."

"Out of all those trucks, why is our convoy the one bracketed?"

Without thinking, I answer, "It's because of me."

Ford faces me and stares.

I sit back and wait to hear the shells come in. There's an old saying, "You never hear the one that's got your name on it."

What the hell am I doing in this shit again? Wasn't Vietnam enough?

My mind blanks as the ground around me erupts. Huge explosions send sand high into the air. I'm not scared, not even worried. No, I'm relaxed, at peace. I begin to recall decisions made many years ago.

Eighteen Years Earlier
12 July 1972

It's two o'clock in the morning. My name is Sergeant Rick Green, United States Marine Corps. I'm lying in bed with my wife, Peg. It's another hot night in our Camp Pendleton base-housing unit. The breeze blowing through the window does little to stop the miserable heat of these summer nights. Suddenly I sit up screaming, "Blood! Look at all the blood!"

Her hands trembling, Peg shakes me. "Wake up, Rick, wake up. You're having another dream."

My eyes are cast down, and my body is covered in sweat.

Slowly I turn and stare at my wife. Moving away, I throw the covers off and sit on the edge of the bed.

Peg gently touches my shoulder. "It's the third time this week. I think they're getting worse."

"They are."

"Can't you find someone on base to help you? Isn't there anyone you can talk to?"

I tell her, "No, Peg, there's no one. If I want to stay in the Corps, I can't let anyone know about these nightmares."

We've talked about me staying in the Corps, or maybe I should say "fought" about it. She wants to go home, I know this. But then she says, "Let me help you. Talk to me about what happened over there. You've never said anything. If things are bothering you, then let me help, please."

I study her, looking for sincerity. "Do you really want to know?" I ask.

"Yes, I do. Come on." Smiling, she holds my hand and rises from the bed. "Let's sit at the kitchen table. I'll make some coffee."

It's difficult for me to start, but once I do, everything pours out. I explain from the beginning how I went from being a naive kid to a stone-cold killer. She listens to every word, wincing at the talk of death, laughing when the stories are funny. While she's sipping hot coffee, her eyes never leave mine.

When I finish, I blurt out what I've done. I don't know why, I just do. "I reenlisted yesterday."

Her expression changes from loving concern to fury. "You promised you were through. You said the Marine Corps was in your past. Why did you do this?"

"What else can I do, Peg? You think the metallurgical job is still there for me? All that awaits me back in Chicago are dead-end jobs for a guy who doesn't even have a high school diploma. I'm good here. I know how to be a Marine. If I leave the Corps, then it's over for me."

Her facial muscles tighten as her tone turns ugly. "You want to stay? Then stay. I'm leaving. And Kimberly is coming with me. You won't see either of us again. Ever!"

I don't know what to say. She's never given me an ultimatum

before. She's never told me to choose between the Corps and my family, my daughter. That night, I make the decision to leave the Marine Corps and go back to Chicago. On 10 December 1972, I'm discharged and heading home.

January 1973

I was paid thirty days' leave when I received my discharge from the Corps. Living in my parents' home has helped me make that money last, but now I need to find a job. I call the plant I worked for before enlisting four years ago. The owner says, "I hired someone as soon as you left, Rick. If I take you back, I'll have to fire him. He's well liked, and I'm not sure how the other employees will feel about you coming back. You understand, don't you?"

Yeah, I understand. I understand I'm not welcome. People in America have turned against us. Young people and the media talk about us being baby killers. I ain't killed any babies. Screw this shit. I'll take care of my family. I don't need anyone.

I miss the Corps. I miss the comradery of fellow Marines. I miss serving. Every day, I'm checking the want ads looking for work. I notice an ad asking for police officers to serve in Sauk Village, a suburb far south of Chicago.

What about being a cop? I could do that job. Hell, I faced people trying to kill me. I know how to use a gun. It's not the Corps, but shit … yeah, man. I'm going to be a cop.

The next day, I arrive at the Sauk Village Police Station, where a test is being given. Inside a room built for fifteen people sit at least twenty-five men. The test is easy. The questions are simple, and I think I'm doing well. When everyone finishes, we're given a second test and told this will count for 50 percent of our grade. On the page are images of faces. We're given about five seconds to study them and then told to turn the page. I'm asked to identify what I saw and find this difficult. I fail that part, which causes me to fail the entire test. My thoughts of being a cop quickly vanish.

I start looking for work again, and within a month, I find a job selling life insurance. The manager of the local office is a

Vietnam vet. He gives me and other vets a chance. After a two-week school, I do pretty well and soon lead the office of thirty-five agents in sales.

With commissions and base pay, my income increases, and I move my small family out of my parents' home into a one-bedroom apartment in the Gage Park area of south Chicago.

I've been free of nightmares these past few months, but they're returning. I may be out of the war, but the war is not out of me. I begin to have flashbacks that send me straight to the jungle. I hear simple everyday things like a helicopter flying over or a car backfiring, and I panic. It becomes so bad, I'm afraid to go anywhere.

It's a hot, sunny Saturday morning in August of '73 when Peg and I take Kimberly to a traveling carnival. I remember how much fun these were when I was a kid and want my daughter to have the same experience. Walking into the fair, I'm like a kid again. "You remember these, Peg?"

"Of course. We had our first date at that one on Archer Avenue."

"Hey, look, cotton candy. Let's get some for Kim," I say. "I don't think she's ever had it before."

We walk over to the vendor selling the candy, my little girl's hand in mine. I let go of her to pay for the treat. While Peg holds Kimberly's hand, I pay for the delicacy and hand it to my daughter. Suddenly from behind comes a loud blast of a Civil War cannon the carnival uses to start the festivities. Some people jump, and Kimberly cries, but most of the people are staring down at me on the ground, my hands over my head.

31 May 1974

This morning, my son, Kevin Michael, is born. Peg and I didn't know if the day would end in joy or pain. After Kimberly was born, Peg's next three pregnancies ended in miscarriages.

When the doctor walks out of the delivery room, he says, "You have a son, Mr. Green." I want to give him a hug. When my eyes fill with tears, the doctor says with a wide grin, "I've never seen the husband cry before." I keep silent, and smile.

January 1975

I'm not doing as well as I was in the insurance business. My sales are down, and my income is dropping. Peg has gotten a job at the local grocery store to help out. I decide to take my license and go out on my own with another agent from the firm. Working out of his home saves us both on rent. I'm now selling exclusively to teachers, and by June, my income is back up once again.

Things between Peg and me turn bad this month. She doesn't need to continue working but says she wants to. I know why she's staying out late and not coming home until early the next morning. Friends tell me rumors of her cheating. One rumor involves a friend we both grew up with. Angry and afraid, I wonder what's happening. Does she not love me? When I was in 'Nam, I worried about her cheating. At first, I had refused to read her letters from home, afraid there was a "Dear John" in them. Now it's happening right in front of me. When I confront her about what people are saying, she confesses everything.

Though it's as I expected, I'm still in shock, and I don't know what to do. I get in my car and drive. I end up at a church. Inside, I kneel at the railing and ask God for help. With no one around, I say out loud, "What do I do, God? Why did she do this? Did I do something to make this happen?" Tears start to flow, and I can't stop them. I put my head down then look up at the cross. I don't say anything. I just stare at Jesus hanging there. My mind goes blank, and I begin to plan my next move. I sniffle in the tears and regain control.

I must leave her. How can I face my friends with everyone knowing what she's done? How can I ever trust her again?

Then I think about my son and daughter. *What am I going to do? My kids. God, please help me.*

I arrive home, and Peggy is sitting on the couch, crying. She tells me it was only once and she'll never do it again.

As before, I choose my kids and forgive her.

30 April 1975

The news is everywhere. Vietnam is under Communist control, and the south surrendered. I'm so depressed, but with many people in this country cheering this news, I stay silent. I feel numb.

All we did over there seems to have been for nothing. All those who died, died for nothing. The thought of an NVA soldier or some VC standing in my hooch at First Recon makes me sick. I want to scream, "Why were we there?"

September 1976

The insurance business went under. I declared bankruptcy, and now I'm driving a truck for a local vending machine company. The pay is good and steady. I move my family out of the small apartment and into a two-bedroom fully furnished mobile home in Gary, Indiana.

Since moving here, Peg and I are doing better. She's met a new friend who lives next door. Her name is Betty, and she's a Mormon. Her religion is a little strange, but having someone godly in Peg's life seems to help our relationship. She's still working but no longer staying out all hours of the night. I think it's going to be a great year.

December 1976

Christmas is right around the corner, and an opportunity for a better job opens up. The post office is hiring and giving veterans an extra five points on a placement test for all new employees. If I can get this job, my time with the Marine Corps will count toward retirement. And I heard I'll begin the job with thirty days a year vacation time, just like in the military.

The testing facility is located on Belmont Street near Western Avenue. That's the north side of Chicago. The test begins at nine o'clock.

I arrive at eight thirty, figuring my promptness will look good to those in charge. I park the car in one of the few spots left in the lot then walk around the corner to the front door. I enter the building and find the place packed. So much for making an early impression. I look for an open seat, and in the corner, I find one. In the seat next to it sits a little guy who reminds me of Bee Bee from back in Recon. I'm thinking he's Marine Corps. I move through the crowded rows and plop down next to him. We both nod but say nothing.

At nine sharp, we're handed a booklet and a pencil. I finally break the ice between us when I ask, "All vets are getting an extra five points on this test, right?"

"That's what I heard. You a vet?" he asks.

"Sure in hell am. Marine Corps."

Smiling, he says, "Semper Fi, brother. Me too."

"No shit, really? My name's Rick, but most guys call me Greeny."

"I'm Bill. You can call me Bubba."

"Really? Bubba. Why Bubba?"

"Picked it up in 'Nam." He adds, "My squad leader's name was Bill, so he said, 'Can't have two Bills in the same team, can ya? We'll call you Bubba.' Or maybe it was because I'm a little round." He pats his belly and shrugs.

"You're a 'Nam vet. So am I. Sixty-nine, seventy."

"Yeah? Sixty-seven, sixty-eight."

"Who were you with?" I ask.

"Twenty-Sixth Marines."

"I was First Recon. You were Khe Sanh, then, huh?"

Nodding, he lets his smile fade, and I know there are memories he doesn't want to think about. I feel for him because we share those same nightmares. "Good luck on the test, man."

"You too, Greeny."

Bubba and I both get the post office jobs. He goes to Chicago, and I go to Indiana. From that day on, Bubba and I are best friends.

July 1977

Over the last nineteen months, I'm in and out of depression. I've been this way since Da Nang fell to the North Vietnamese two years ago. It's worse now, and I'm not sure why. I try to hide it but cannot. Bubba and I talk about what happened there. We're both bothered by it, and he feels the same as me, mad as hell.

I quit the post office to try college. I want to be a computer programmer, but my plan to get an education isn't working. I don't seem to have the drive, and I have a family to support. Sometimes I want to run away. Nothing seems to interest me. Sometimes I feel I'm just holding on, and my mind takes me to dark places.

I took a job as a meat-cutter apprentice. There's good pay learning to be a butcher. I'm starting to feel better about myself and have no more bad thoughts. I hope it stays that way.

Peg is cheating again. She started work yesterday at six in the evening. Her shift ended at eleven, but she didn't get home until four in the morning, telling me they kept her late to do inventory. This has been going on for a couple of months now. Once again, as before, it all comes to a head when I catch her in the lie and threaten to leave. She cries and promises, once again, to stop. With a son and daughter to consider, I have to give our relationship another try. That night, we make passionate, forgiving love.

Things have settled down between us, but we're not the same. We sell the mobile home and buy a little three-bedroom place in Hammond, Indiana. In March of '79, another child is born, a baby girl, Kathleen. She's my little angel.

Peg had quit her job before Kathleen was born but informs me she'll be returning to work at the same store.

The nightmares from Vietnam over the last seven years are less frequent now. I still occasionally have one, but I've learned to handle them. I'm quiet these days. Not sure if Peg even notices. Not sure she ever notices me. Something else is on my mind, something that has always been there. Approaching thirty soon, I'm running out of time. I want to be a Marine again.

April 1979

The weather is nice, a sunny spring day in the fifties. After our harsh winter, it feels warm and exciting. I'm close to home when I decide to make a detour. There on the corner is the Marine Corps recruiter. I stop in. The office is filled with Marine Corps posters and paraphernalia. A staff sergeant, still in his winter uniform of long-sleeve khaki shirt and tie, sits behind a large brown desk. We talk for a while, but I never tell him what I'm thinking. We only chat about the Corps and days gone by.

I think he senses my true purpose for being there when he tells me the Marine Corps is accepting prior service Marines into the reserves. He asks, "You ever considered reenlisting?"

I'm silent but excited at the thought. "Not sure I ever could. I've got a wife and three kids," I reply as if it's a question, hoping to get the answer that I can join.

"The reserves are hurting for Marines. I'll look into it. See if they're taking prior service with families. Like yourself."

I'm excited. The thought of being a Marine again grows inside me.

31 October 1979

Halloween night and I'm taking my three little ones trick-or-treating. Peggy's not here. I'm not sure where she is, but she's cheating again. She's doing what she wants without worrying about what it's doing to our marriage.

CHAPTER 2

1980

I'VE LOST THREE JOBS SINCE the year began, all due to layoffs. In November I start a new job, driving a bread truck. I'm in a union and the pay is decent, not great, but I can catch up on my mortgage. It's three months in arrears. If it falls any further behind, the bank will start foreclosure.

It's been eight years since I left the Marine Corps. I've forgotten much about that time in my life. By choice, maybe, I don't know. I just don't think about it anymore. Not remembering makes my life easier.

It's Saturday, and Bubba and I are meeting for dinner and drinks. We try to get together once a month, something we both look forward to. I had to trade Peggy two Saturdays of her time just to get this one night a month. Seems like I'm always giving more.

Bubba lives in Chicago and likes to come over to Indiana. We usually go to his favorite seafood place, Phil Smidt's in Whiting. Afterward, we stop at this dive on Calumet Avenue for a few beers. Bubba has put on a few pounds since I met him. He's still not fat, but he's definitely gotten rounder. He says he weighs one hundred eighty pounds, but he's five eight, so I don't know.

Bubba has told me often about his time with the Twenty-Sixth Marines and Khe Sanh. He was there from the beginning of the siege until the end, including the battle to retake Hill 881. His stories are hairy. I was in 'Nam later than him, but Bubba never tells me he had it rougher than me. We both know, once a man's seen combat, it doesn't matter how much or where. All combat veterans are brothers in arms.

The dive we stop at is quiet for a Saturday night. The place is loaded with World War II and Korea veterans and is usually friendly. That doesn't mean Vietnam vets are welcome. Even after this many years, some of these veterans don't like us for the way the war ended.

Bubba and I are minding our own business and just sitting at the bar. This Army guy starts telling us how, when he was in Korea, he saw more action than anything we did in Vietnam. Two biker guys, who look like they came out of a sixties movie starring Peter Fonda, are with him. They start complaining to the bartender, "This bar is for real veterans, not those who lose a war."

I tell Bubba, "Let's di di mau, man." Bubba and I get up and head for the door. Then the Army puke opens his mouth one more time. "You people are the only ones to lose an American war. You're an embarrassment to veterans. You're all a bunch of cowards."

Bubba isn't real big about a lot of things, but calling him and the friends he lost in 'Nam "cowards" is too much. He walks up to the Korean vet and lays him out with one punch to the jaw. The asshole falls off his stool and hits the floor like a sack of potatoes. His biker friends jump on Bubba, and I jump on them, and we have us an old-fashioned barroom brawl. I'm hitting people I don't know, and it doesn't matter. If I see a face, I hit it. They get a few licks in on me. We fight until we hear a loud gunshot. Bubba and I half hit the floor. It's over.

The bartender holds a double-barrel shotgun with smoke curling out one barrel. "That was a blank," he says. "The next barrel is buckshot, enough to cover this entire room. Now y'all clear the hell out. The cops are on the way. Y'all get on home. Now!"

Bubba and I take off for my car.

"That was great, Bubba. I ain't done something like that in a long time."

"Me neither, Greeny."

As we drive, I have to ask, "Hey, Bubba, you miss it?"

"Miss what, man?"

"The Corps. You miss being in the Marine Corps? Miss all the shit that goes down. You know, miss the big Green Weenie."

Bubba stares at me as if I'm nuts. Finally, he answers, "Sometimes … but no, man. You know, once a Marine…" Then we say in unison, "Always a Marine." We laugh.

I shock Bubba when I say, "I'm reenlisting."

"What the fuck. Are you crazy? You're married, with three kids?"

"Yeah, man, I know. But I was always supposed to be a lifer. It's what I always wanted. It's in my blood, Bubba. I never stop thinking about it. I need to be back in the Corps."

I'm looking for approval. I need someone to tell me what I'm about to do is okay. He gazes out his window.

"I can go back in and get the rank of corporal. My time in grade starts at day one, but I'll be a Marine again."

He turns back to me. "What the hell, Greeny. Where you going to be stationed?"

"I can't go active. I'll be reserve. They have a unit in Gary, Indiana. It's close to home, and I'll be in Motor Transport. OJT, man. Learn to drive the big rigs."

He smiles. "On the job training. What's Peg say?"

I pull up in front of the East Chicago station where Bubba catches the train home. "I ain't said anything to her yet. But man, things aren't real good between us. She's cheating on me again."

"Really, man? Shit, I'm sorry, dude. I thought all that was behind you two."

"Yeah, well, ain't nothin' but a thing." He gives me the look that he gets it, and he gets me. "So whatever she wants to do, she can do. I can't live my life in fear she's going to leave me anymore. I've lost so much time trying to keep us together. If I don't do this now, I'll never do it. It's my last chance."

Bubba and I exchange a glance. He puts his hand behind my neck and says, "You'll make a great lifer, man." He gets out and walks up the stairs to the platform. The train arrives, and I watch him leave.

I drive away realizing I'm going to have to tell Peg my plans, but not yet. First I'm going to get signed up and accepted into the Marines.

Early Sunday morning, I get a call from Bubba's brother, Charlie. Crying, he tells me, "My brother's dead. Billy was beaten and stabbed to death last night."

CHAPTER 3

STARTING OVER

23 January 1980

WEDNESDAY IS MY DAY OFF. It's nine o'clock. I pull my car into the parking lot of Phillips Funeral Home on the south side of Chicago. A man dressed in a dark suit and carrying a clipboard approaches my vehicle. "Are you friend or family?" he asks.

"I'm a friend."

"What's your name, sir?"

"Rick Green."

He checks his list and sticks a gold shield on my car window. "Park on the right side, please, Mr. Green. The family has asked for you to be a pallbearer."

I nod but don't speak. This is an unexpected honor.

Inside the funeral parlor are several people I don't know. I've never met his brother Charlie or his mother, Evelyn. After walking to the front of the room, I stand and look down at my best friend lying in a casket. He's wearing a blue suit. Bubba hated suits. I know he'd rather be in blue jeans and a jacket.

Should I say a prayer to God for you, man? Don't think you cared much about that stuff, my friend. God, if you're there, give me a clear shot at whoever did this.

I bend over to Bubba's ear and whisper, "Hey, Bub, they fixed your skull, man, where they broke it open. It looks better. Your bruises are gone, too. Hey, they fixed your nose. Looks better than when you were alive." I snicker. "I talked to Owens, you know, the coroner detective from Lake County. He got ahold of the detectives in Calumet City. It's their jurisdiction. They told him not all the blood on your clothes was yours. Guess you gave as good as you got. If they find out who did this, Bubba, you know what I'll do."

A hand touches my shoulder, and I straighten. It's my friend's mother.

"Billy loved you, Rick. You know that, don't you?" She speaks in a soft, trembling voice. Her eyes fill with tears.

"Yes, ma'am, Mrs. Balding. I know. I love him too." I can say no more. If I do, the emotions will overwhelm me, and I don't want to cry.

She smiles. "I know all his friends called him Bubba, but to me, he's my Billy." Her gaze wanders away as she tries to remember. "When did that start, Rick? Calling him Bubba." Looking back at me, she says, "I think it was in Vietnam. Maybe that was where."

"Yes, ma'am, I think that's what Bubba told me."

Unable to hold back her tears, she starts to cry. Her voice breaks as she says, "My son went through hell in Vietnam. I know because I still hear his cries at night." Gazing deep into my eyes, she says, "He never told me what happened to him, over there." She sounds desperate. "I tried to get him to talk about it, Rick. I really did." Then with a half smile, she tells me what Bubba said to her. "Marines don't bitch, Mom. We hack it."

With a steady eye, I maintain a hard-fought self-control. I understand what Bubba was saying.

Another family member comes to her and offers condolences, and she walks away.

I stay for the family's traditional lunch. Afterward I say my goodbyes and head out. Sitting in my car, I take a second to reflect, put the key in, and start the engine. I pull onto Archer Avenue then drive west toward I-55. The interstate is traffic-free this time of day, and in no time, I'm on I-94 and heading for Indiana, leaving Chicago behind.

Man. That was brutal. What do I do now, Bubba? Tears I held back at the funeral start filling my eyes.

Bubba understood my pain, and I understood his. Our visits on

16

Saturday nights might find us getting so drunk that he would spend the night on my couch. We'd share stories about Vietnam, laughing our asses off at the funny shit. We'd listen to each other when the stories got tense and cry over the rest. We shared condolences over buddies we lost. Bubba had a lot of those memories. When he got drunk, his stories came easier.

He remembered a lot about Hill 881 and the Khe Sanh siege in 1968. Dreams still haunted him. I remember one he told me many times. He said he'd hunkered down in a bunker, waiting to die, thinking the next NVA 122-millimeter rocket had his name on it. The screams of the dead and dying became too much.

Yeah, Bubba and me, we'd just hold onto each other. Now he's gone, and I'm alone. *Why the hell did you die, you dumb ass?*

Tears burn down my face, my emotions unchecked. I pull over to the side of the road. Leaning my head against the steering wheel, I let everything pour out until I'm whimpering. Anger takes over, and I scream, "Damn you, Bubba! Why didn't you fight harder? Why didn't you live?" I regain composure and understand that my friend fought as hard as he could. I pull the car back on the road and head home.

Hey, Bubba, ain't nothin' but a thing. I'm glad your pain is finally over.

Peg and I have been married eleven years. With three kids, we've had good times and bad, but I know Peg isn't happy now. And I'm about to drop a bombshell.

Walking through the back door, I stomp the excess snow off my boots. Our home in Hammond, Indiana, is tiny. It has this kitchen, a living room, and three small bedrooms.

Peg doesn't look up from the sink while doing dishes. "How was the funeral? Did you have lunch?"

"Yeah, his family had some food at a local restaurant, I'm good."

She stops washing and looks at me over her shoulder. "You okay?"

"Yeah, I'm fine." I sit on a kitchen chair and start removing

17

my boots. "I thought they'd have a flag or something. They didn't have anything remembering what he did for this country. Nothing. Not a damn thing."

While scrubbing hard on the bottom of a frying pan, she smirks. "What did you expect?"

I ignore her. "Are you going to work tonight?"

"Yeah, Janice called and told me to come in at six. She said she needs me to stay late again."

"How late, Peg? It seems she wants you to stay late every night. She has you working until two or three every morning."

Janice, recently divorced, is Peg's boss. She owns the local convenience store a few blocks from our home. I suspect these late nights involve more than just working.

"Are you at least going to be home before I have to go to work?"

Clearly angry, she raises her voice. "I don't know. Look, you wanted me to get a job, so I got one. I'm at work when you're home with the kids. I'm always here before you have to leave."

"No, you're not. I can't be late for work again. Last week, I waited thirty minutes for you to get home. I sped all the way in and still punched in five minutes late."

"You want me to quit? I'll quit."

I yell back, "Okay, quit!"

"I'm not quitting! We need the money, and I like the job."

That's when I blurt out, "I'm going back in the Marine Corps."

Peg jerks around, her hands still dripping soapy water. "What the hell are you talking about?" Her eyes open wide, and her face turns red. "If you think for one fucking minute I'm following you around this country or anywhere else while you go play soldier..."

With boots off, I stand and face her. "Look, I'm not going anywhere. I'm enlisting in the reserves. It's one weekend a month, and most of those weekends, I'll be home at night. There's a two-week annual training time away from home once a year, but that's it."

She calms down. Her mouth draws into a little smile as she warms up to the idea. "Okay. Maybe that's okay. I know you always wanted to be back in the Marines, so this is okay. When are you signing up?"

The tone of her voice is soft, and she's no longer angry. I have a hunch she's getting exactly what she wants.

"Next week. I'm signing up next week."

23 January 1980

I'm at the Marine Corps recruiting office in Hammond, Indiana. I've stopped here before, always checking on the possibility of going back into the service. The last time was only a few days before Bubba and I met for our last drink together.

I walk into the office. Staff Sergeant Leroy Jones sits behind his desk. Jones is a Marine of color and is wearing his dress blues trousers with the blood stripe down the side. His long-sleeve khaki shirt is perfectly pressed. I look down at his ribbons and badges over his left breast pocket, and they too are in perfect order.

"Hey, Green. How you doing? Think any more about coming back in?" He smiles broadly.

Pictures of his wife and child sit at the corner of his desk. In the center is a desktop monthly calendar. Written across the bottom is the Marine Corps motto, *Semper Fidelis*. On the wall behind him is a photo of his graduating class from Staff NCO Academy, and another photo of his Career Recruiter Course class is hung right next to it. Plastered on the walls of the office are several other small recruiting posters. Even though I'm still a civilian, I remain standing until invited to sit. "That's what I'm about to do, Staff Sergeant."

"Sit. Sit," he offers.

I sit on the edge of one of the two matching high-back black leather chairs in front of his desk. I lay one hand on his desk and ask, "Everything still the same? I get the rank of corporal and assignment to Motor Transport?"

He reaches to a side cabinet and takes out a file folder and places it in front of me on the desk. He opens the folder and removes a single sheet of paper. I look at it, surprised to see it's filled in with my information. All that's missing is the date and my signature.

"All you need to do is sign and date it. Then we get everything moving."

"A single sheet? That's it?"

"It's a lot different for prior service. This is a request for records from Headquarters Marine Corps. All the heavy paperwork will be done by the company."

While signing, I ask, "They're located in Gary, right?"

"Like I told you, they're right by the lake in good old Gary, Indiana."

"So what happens now?"

"Now I fax this to Marine Corps Headquarters and send a copy to Support Company. I'll arrange for them to get their Navy doctor to give you a physical. The company CO will have to accept you, but that won't be a problem. You'll be back in uniform by March. They drill on the first weekend of the month, Green. Keep that time open."

20 February 1980

It's Wednesday and my day off. I'm sitting at home watching television when Jones calls. "Hey, Green. Support Company is never going to get a doctor on a drill weekend. Your record book is sitting in Admin waiting for you. The company CO and Motor Transport Platoon both want you. Everything's good to go except for this damn physical. I want to send you to MEPS. It's our best shot. I can get you in on Monday, April tenth."

"Back to the Military Entrance Processing Station? Are you kidding, Staff Sergeant?"

"That's our best hope of getting you in before the Marine Corps puts a stop on OJT for prior service."

A bit concerned, I ask, "Is that happening?"

"Those are the rumors I'm hearing, so let's get this done ASAP."

"Copy that."

On April 10, paperwork in hand, I leave for MEPS. Jones said I'll cruise right through the lines and straight to the doctor. That's how it should go. But the last thing I need is to get caught up in what's known as the fuck-up of military bullshit. That's when one hand has no idea what the other hand is doing.

It's 0530 when I walk through the door off Polk Street, the same street I entered from in 1968. This time, I expect things to go much quicker. I get in a line leading to a table staffed by two enlisted service members. One is Army and the other Navy. The two seem to be in no hurry to move the line along, and my patience is wearing thin. When it's my turn, I hand them a folder with my paperwork. The Army PFC grabs it and gives me a look that says I'm some kind of asshole by handing in only two sheets of paper.

"Where's the rest of your paperwork, recruit?" he asks.

"First off, I'm not a recruit, and second, that's all I have."

Looking over what I've given him, he checks his list of names. "You're not a recruit? So what are you?"

I try to cover my disdain. "Prior service."

"You're not on my list."

"What the hell do you mean? My paperwork is right there in your hand."

The PFC glares at the clipboard. "You're not on the list. I can't send you on if you're not on the list."

I'm pissed. After several minutes of back-and-forth, I demand to see his superior.

Talk about dysfunctional.

A Marine staff sergeant walks over, and I explain my situation. Everything gets straightened out, and I take my physical. With the results in hand, I leave MEPS behind and head to the recruiter's office. With Staff Sergeant Jones in possession of the results of my physical, I go home and wait for him to call.

My part is done. The next step: drill weekend.

CHAPTER 4

HERE I GO AGAIN

10 May 1980

I'VE BEEN UP FOR HOURS and am anxious to leave for my first drill weekend. Soon, I'll be back in the Marine Corps.

Staff Sergeant Jones reminded me to wait until after 0800 before reporting in. He said to check only into Admin and Supply. I know he doesn't want me hanging around while the company is going through formation. It's best if I arrive when they're all working and ready for me.

Zero seven hundred finally arrives, and I'm off. The sky is cloudy and the air is cool and damp, but I don't think it will rain. The trip down on a Saturday morning takes less than thirty minutes since the traffic is light on I-94. I connect with I-65 and head north to US-20/12 then east to Lake Street. A left-hand turn toward the beach and then a few more blocks, and the reserve center is on my left.

Two double commercial-size cyclone gates stand wide-open and unguarded, unlike any military base I've been on. Off the gates is a cyclone fence that seems to encircle the entire compound. The lot is filled with older-model autos. Some are rusted so bad they look as if they're held together with baling twine and paper clips.

This must be enlisted parking. How'd these beaters get anywhere?

I check the time, and it's 0735. With time to kill, I scope out the area. A single-story building in front of me looks as if it's made of tin. It's not very large, and from what I can tell, it's only a few hundred square feet. Staff Sergeant Jones mentioned I should go to the headquarters building in front of the enlisted parking.

Protruding blocks of charred rubble are along the side of the building. An open area to my right has loose stones and the remains of a foundation with pipes sticking out.

Evidence of some kind of fire here. Jones never mentioned that. Worry about it later. I gotta check in. What's the time? Zero seven forty-five. Close enough for government work.

I smile and slide out of my car, close the door, and walk toward headquarters. A mechanical shop sits beyond the open lot, and two large bay doors in the front are closed. Several plain white mobile homes are scattered around the complex. I spot a few Marines entering one of them.

There's definitely been some damage here. There was a building there, and I'll bet those mobile homes are temporary classrooms.

I walk through the front door and down a hallway leading to a huge room. I pause and wonder how I misjudged the size of this place. From the outside, the building looked small. From inside, I see a thousand-square-foot area.

Marines are hustling about in all directions. With so many voices chattering, the conversations are unintelligible. Along the sides of the room are several partitioned cubicles with Marines working inside. Three permanent offices line the back wall.

Those must be for the CO, XO, and I'll bet ... the first sergeant.

Marines are working at a line of desks running down the middle of the room. I walk up to the closest one and say, "I'm looking for Admin."

The PFC at the desk points at one of the partitioned areas along the back wall. "Over there, sir. That's Admin."

I move across the floor to the partitioned site, and inside sits a sergeant attending to another Marine. I stand and wait.

When finished, the sergeant asks, "What can I do for you, sir?"

I step up to his desk. "I'm Corporal Green reporting in today." The nameplate on his desk reads Sergeant Mallon, Admin Chief. I estimate he's not more than twenty years old. After he takes my paperwork, he offers me a seat on the only other chair in the office.

"I had to pull some strings to get you in this company, Corporal," Sergeant Mallon says.

"What do you mean, 'pull some strings'?"

"A Marine Corps order came down effective April one. It said there will be no more OJT for Motor Transport." He stops and looks up at me. "From that point on, every MOS will be school-trained." He stares at me for a moment then looks back at his work. "But some people in this company want you here." Another pause. "I'm told in no uncertain terms to make it happen."

I'm confused. I don't know anyone here. I haven't even met the CO or XO. I ask, "What people are you talking about, Sergeant?"

He stamps my papers and tells me, "You're finished here. Take this to Supply." He hands me a chit for what I need and says, "Report to Motor Transport Platoon. Staff Sergeant Baylor is the Motor Transport chief. You'll find Supply and him across the lot in the maintenance building."

"Copy that, Sergeant. Is that the building with the bay doors?"

He nods, and I'm off.

Outside, I head across the lot and find a side door on the left. Walking inside, I hear the clang of metal on metal, and the smell of oil fills the air. Marines are working on a jeep on one side, and on the other side is a Dutch door. The lower hatchway is closed, and the upper is open. Above the hatch is the word "Supply."

A lance corporal sits inside at a desk, reading a book.

"I'm checking in, Lance Corporal."

Without a word, he looks up at me, puts down the book, stands, and moves to the hatchway. He takes my chit, hands me a form, and tells me to fill out all my sizes. The form has a picture of a man with trousers, a cover, belt, boots—everything, including my rank. I do as he asks then give it back. After receiving one pair of boots and two of everything else, I'm now in possession of a full green camouflaged United States Marine Corps utility uniform.

"You want me to cut your belt down to size for you, Corporal?"

The webbed belts never come in the right size, and his offer to cut it will allow me to dress and wear it today. "Thanks, Lance Corporal. I'll size it." It takes several minutes for me to figure out how long the belt needs to be. When I'm done, I give it back to him, and he cuts it down.

I walk everything over to headquarters, where I find a head with enough room to change clothes. Dressed in my Marine Corps uniform, I look in the mirror and feel a sense of pride and embarrassment. Pride because I'm back in the Corps, embarrassment because my uniform looks like shit. Even though the belt fits, the brass buckle is dull and dirty. My boots have no shine at all. I look like a first-phase boot. But wearing my corporal chevrons makes me feel good.

I stow my civilian gear in my POV, or Privately Owned Vehicle, and walk across the lot to the maintenance building. The warm May sun shines on my face as it shows itself from behind the morning clouds. The bay doors of the maintenance building are open.

A truck is in the middle bay and the jeep still in the other. I walk in where the truck is. A PFC is sitting on a stool, working on a tire still attached to the vehicle.

"Where can I find Staff Sergeant Baylor?" I ask.

"Up those stairs, in the office, Corporal."

"Thanks."

A set of stairs is on my right, against the back wall, and at the top is a door with a window. Inside, I can see the heads of a few Marines at work. I walk up the steps. A sign on the door reads "Knock," so I do.

Someone inside yells, "Enter."

I push the door open. At least half a dozen Marines from the rank of staff sergeant down to lance corporal are in this office. Staffs are sitting at gray military desks at the far end of the room, while others are standing around.

I announce, "I'm looking for Staff Sergeant Baylor."

From the other side of the room, a Marine stands. "I'm Baylor. Are you Green?"

"Yes, Staff Sergeant, I'm Corporal Green, reporting in."

Smiling, Baylor says, "I've been expecting you. Front and center, Green." I walk to his desk, and he greets me. "You all checked in?"

"Yes, Staff Sergeant."

Looking me over, he says, "That uniform needs to be squared away by tomorrow."

"Copy that, Staff Sergeant. I'll square it away tonight."

Baylor walks around his desk and orders, "Follow me, Green." I follow him to a window. He stands a little shorter than me and is balding. We're about the same age, which makes him Vietnam era. Perhaps he and I will talk about that later.

"How's your day going, Corporal? Good so far?" Baylor's smile grows, almost turning to laughter. Looking around the room, I can't help noticing everyone's eyes are on me. They're in a chipper mood. I have a feeling I'm the brunt of some unknown joke.

With hesitation, I answer, "Yeah, Staff Sergeant, I'm good to go."

"That's good. I'm glad to hear it." He looks out the window and points at a group of all-black Marines standing in the sunshine. "You see that cluster of Marines down there? Those dark-green Marines? That group right there?"

I see the group he means. They're smoking, laughing, and seem to be, well, trouble. "Yes, Staff Sergeant, I do."

"You see them? Them, right there? That's first squad." He turns and looks into my eyes. "That's your squad. Welcome aboard."

CHAPTER 5

IT'S A DIFFERENT MARINE CORPS

A S I LOOK DOWN AT those Marines, I'm reminded of the racial tension I experienced at firebase An Hoa in Vietnam. "So, what's the deal, Staff Sergeant? Who are they?" Snickers of laughter carry through the office. I don't smile.

Baylor moves away from the window and parks himself on the front of his desk. Another staff sergeant who is sitting close by says, "They call themselves The Crowd." I look at him, my patience running thin.

He spouts off, "What's the matter, Green? You don't get it, do you?"

Tension builds inside of me. Then I catch sight of two bobblehead dolls standing on top of a gray filing cabinet behind the staff sergeant. I smile. One is of President Jimmy Carter, and the other is the person who wants his job this November, Ronald Reagan.

The staff sergeant also smiles. "You like my bobbleheads, Corporal?"

"Yeah, Staff Sergeant, I do." His uniform is well pressed, and his hair is Marine Corps regulation. His neatly arranged desk tells me he's a diligent office manager.

"You have a question, ask," he says.

I glance around the room at the other Marines who are still staring at me, until they catch the eyes of both staff sergeants. They return to their work. Looking back at Staff Sergeant Baylor, I ask, "So, those Marines down there, they don't listen to anyone?

They just do their own thing? Is that the joke?" I take a moment to consider what I'm about to ask next. "Is this a racial thing?"

Baylor stops grinning. "Racial? No, not on our part. Maybe theirs. Maybe a little. But that's not the biggest problem you have to deal with."

Frustrated, I ask, "I'll have to deal with? What's going on? What aren't you telling me?"

"Okay, Green, okay. Here it is. You've been out of the Corps for a few years, and you've never been in a reserve unit." He stands up and moves behind his desk. "You listen to the news? You know how the military is being downsized?"

"Yeah, I get that."

He picks up a Marine Corps coffee mug from his desk and swallows the last gulp. "When all the services are being cut, what do you think happens to the Corps?" He steps back to refill his coffee cup then sits at his desk, waiting for an answer that doesn't come. "We get the scraps, and the Marine Corps reserve gets the leftovers." With a big fake smile, he adds, "Guess what? There ain't anything left over." He sets his coffee down. "Shit, did you see that jeep in the bay down there?"

"Yeah," I answer.

"I bet you think we're trying to fix it, right?"

I shrug, not sure what he wants me to think.

"Two drill weekends ago, we had to push it into the bay. With nothing else to do, the mechanics take it apart and put it back together, just to keep busy. You see that six-by truck in the bay next to the jeep? That, Corporal, is the only truck on this base that still runs. We don't drive it, though. We've stripped the parts off every other truck to keep it running. We can't get parts to fix any of our vehicles. Does it look familiar to you? It should. It's Vietnam era." He laughs. "Even if we did have parts, we haven't had any diesel fuel for..." He yells across the room. "Hey, Sergeant Tabor, when was the last time we had a fuel delivery?"

"You want an exact date or approximate, Staff Sergeant?"

"Don't be a smart-ass. Tell me how long ago."

"More than six months, Staff Sergeant."

Baylor looks at me. "Tabor is our bulk fuel NCO. He doesn't have much to do these days. You see, Green, even if our trucks weren't deadline, we wouldn't have any fuel to run them. If we went to war today, there would be no equipment for supporting any operation. None."

Baylor leans back in his chair and, locking his fingers behind his head, tells me, "Grab a chair, Corporal. It's not just our platoon. It's the whole damn company. Heavy equipment has one bulldozer, and it's from 1948. We can't use it. It doesn't work."

I begin to realize the Marine Corps I left is not the one I'm in today. I find a folding chair leaning against the wall and place it in front of Baylor's desk and sit. "So what's up with first squad? What aren't you telling me?"

"They've lost esprit de corps. They have no respect for anyone or anything. They've been screwed over too many times. If it wasn't for the threat of a dishonorable discharge, they'd be gone. They're not the only ones. In our platoon, Marines come to drill and sit around doing nothing. We have them PM vehicles they know will never run. We should be out running convoys, not sitting in classrooms every drill weekend. Young Marines report in from their Motor T school and never drive a vehicle. I've never seen morale so low." Baylor grimaced.

"All that is bad, but it's not our biggest problem. The biggest problem is pay. The enlisted ranks haven't been paid for several months. One Marine in first squad, Lance Corporal Harris, has gone a year without pay. What makes this even more difficult is when the upper rank's pay comes through like clockwork. Only the E5s and below have the glitches. With the economy so fucked up, they depend on those checks to survive, so now, some of them don't have gas money to make drill."

What the fuck did I get myself into?

While trying to hide my frustration, I ask, "So why do you want me to be their squad leader?"

The other staff sergeant weighs in. "When you applied to the company, Corporal, I got your record book. I sat down with Staff Sergeant Baylor, and you fit our platoon perfectly. We need you because of your prior service, because you're a Vietnam vet, a Recon Marine, and you saw action in 'Nam."

"So you think with all that, I can snap those guys into being good Marines? I don't think so. That's not going to work."

Baylor turns to the other staff sergeant then looks back at me. "Staff Sergeant Harden and I don't expect you to do that. We're looking for someone with your maturity and your experience to get the Marines in first squad on track. And bring some enthusiasm and esprit de corps to the rest of the platoon." Baylor pauses and stares for a moment while I'm still unsure what they expect of me. "Circumstances and the times we're living in have put undue pressure on these Marines. I'm hoping someone like you can help turn this around."

"What is it you expect me to do?"

"With your example, bring back pride. Pride in the Corps. Those Marines had it once, but not anymore."

Staff Sergeant Harden jumps in. "I'm I and I, Corporal. I'm from the regular side of the house, and I've seen this happening at Camp Pendleton too. The regulars struggle with pride in the Corps too. With all the bullshit these days, it's hard for young Marines to stay focused."

"I and I? What's that?" I ask.

Staff Sergeant Baylor laughs. "You do have a lot to learn, Green. When we finish here, I want you to go over to Admin and enroll in some MCI courses. Learn everything there is to know about Motor Transport."

"And what's MCI, Staff?"

Baylor looks over at Harden, who shakes his head in obvious disbelief. "Come on, Green, don't you grunts know anything? MCI, Marine Corps Institute. As far as I and I, listen up. That stands for Inspector and Instructor. I'm in charge of Motor T, and Staff Sergeant Harden is my active duty counterpart, I and I. Understood?"

"I think so."

Staff Sergeant Hayden explains, "I'm the same MOS as Staff Sergeant Baylor. In the regulars, I'm a Motor T chief, just like

Baylor is here. When you people are gone for the month, I keep everything in order for your return on drill weekend. It's my job to train Staff Sergeant Baylor in the event this unit is activated for war. Now do you understand?"

"Yeah, I get it. So, Staff Sergeant Baylor, you're in charge of me during the drill weekend?"

"Yes. I make the decisions. We don't have a lieutenant, so I'm also the acting platoon commander. Understood?"

I nod.

"If you have no more questions, Green, you're dismissed. Go over to Admin and get set up with the MCI classes. You're going to need to learn as much about Motor T as possible. Formation goes tonight at twenty hundred hours."

"Copy that, Staff Sergeant."

With a few hours left until formation, I make my way to headquarters to see about those MCI courses. If I understood Baylor, they will all be home study.

Along the way, I think about what the two staff sergeants told me they hoped I would bring to the platoon. It's flattering but also close to impossible.

Somehow I have to gain respect of Marines whose only reason for being here is to do their time and receive an honorable discharge. How can I get them to snap to it if there's no discipline? Writing a Marine up for disobeying orders doesn't do any good. Why would a Marine care if he gets office hours? So what if the commanding officer finds them guilty and orders loss of pay, which he isn't receiving, anyway.

No, the only way to run this unit is through respect for the Marine giving the orders.

How the hell am I going to gain the respect of these Marines?

After finishing up in Admin, I take a quick look at the clock, and it reminds me it's almost time for final formation. I've not yet met my squad, and I'm both anxious and nervous. I arrive and find the platoon in formation. At the head of first squad stands a huge Marine at least six inches taller than me. He would have no

31

problem snapping me in half. His rank is lance corporal, and I assume he's been the acting squad leader.

"I'm Corporal Green, your new squad leader. What's your name, Lance Corporal?"

He lowers his head, his eyes filled with resentment. His manner doesn't change from the expression it has held since I stood in front of him. He's bitter.

I've faced an NVA bullet and seen the death of war. I know what fear is, and I must admit, that's what I feel. I hold steadfast to show I don't fear as I wait for his answer. Seconds go by as we continue to stare at one another, and I'm not sure if he's going to answer me or crush me, but I don't flinch. I don't even blink. Finally, he answers, "Harris."

This is the Marine who hasn't been paid for a year.

"Move the squad down one man, Lance Corporal."

He continues to stare down at me, not moving or talking, only staring. I imagine he's wondering, "What does this white boy think he's doing in my squad?" Then in a low, commanding tone, he orders, "Y'all move down one. Hurry up."

The squad follows his orders, and one by one they all move, making room for me at its head. I step in line for my first Marine Corps formation since 1972. The Corps may have changed. Things may be different, but I'm back, and tomorrow will be day two in this new Marine Corps.

CHAPTER 6

DIRTY LITTLE SECRETS

O N MY WAY HOME, I stop at Walmart for items I need in order to get ready for tomorrow. My purchases include a can of Brasso polish, a clothing marking kit, and a tin of Lincoln black boot polish. It's ten o'clock when I walk through the back of my darkened house. The light from a flickering television at a low volume comes from the living room. *Sounds like Peg's awake.*

A teenage girl sleeps on the sofa.

"Who are you?" My voice is loud and abrupt.

She jumps awake. "Sorry, Mr. Green. I-I-I'm the babysitter."

Harsher, I say, "Where are the kids? And where's my wife?"

She trembles as she responds. "Th-the children are all asleep. In bed. Your wife is at work … I think."

You ass, you're scaring her.

I wasn't angry with the girl. I took a deep breath—in and out—to find some control.

"What's your name?"

"Carol." The teenager is still trembling.

I soften my tone. "How much do I owe you, Carol?"

"Ten dollars, sir."

I hand her a ten and a five as an apology for my reaction. "Can you get home okay?"

"Yes, sir. I live on the next block. I'll cut through your yard, if that's okay?"

"Sure, go ahead."

She slips into a high school letter-sweater and hustles out the back. After the door closes behind her, I watch through a window until she clears the back gate.

The kids, asleep in their beds when I check on them, look so peaceful. I move to each child, touching an arm or a hand as a wordless good night. I close their doors and walk to my bedroom. After I strip to my skivvies and T-shirt, I prepare for Sunday's drill.

With the Brasso, I start polishing the buckle and the tip of the web belt until both shine as they did when I was in boot camp. Next, I get out the iron and ironing board. I adjust the heat knob so the iron is at its highest temperature. Frustrated, I press hard on the cloth, attempting to remove every wrinkle from my uniform, making it as close to perfection as possible. Finally, I place my corporal chevrons on the collar in flawless alignment.

My boots are next. I spit-polish the shine until I can see to comb my hair in the gleaming toe. Lastly, I take the stamping kit and affix each letter of my last name and initials to the stamp section. After applying the ink, I carefully place it above the left breast pocket and press down evenly until my name clearly appears.

I lay the uniform on my bed. Cover on top, blouse, belt, and trousers. Boots sit on the floor below them. I look at the items with pride. *Everything is good to go.* Carefully, I hang the uniform and check the clock. It's nearly two in the morning, and I'm ready for day two.

Peg is still not home.

My need to grab some sleep forces me to go to bed, but instead of sleep, worrisome thoughts invade my mind. I stare at the ceiling. *It's what I expected.*

It's Sunday morning. The store she works at and all the bars are closed. I can only imagine where she is, who she's with. I try not to care. Somehow I fall asleep. At four thirty I'm awake, and Peg is lying next to me. I wonder how long she's been there. I'm up and dressed and on my way before five o'clock.

11 May 1980

I arrive at the drill center and park in the same lot as the day before. At 0530 the lot is empty, so I have my choice of where to park. I decide to find a space as close to the headquarters building as possible. I walk the hundred yards from my car to the maintenance building, carrying a notepad. A warm morning breeze on my face adds to the promise of a summerlike day.

From the bay area, I notice a light shining in the upstairs window. Inside the office, Staff Sergeant Baylor stands at the coffeepot as it percolates. "Morning, Staff Sergeant."

He looks over. "Hey, Green, you're here early."

"Thought I'd come in to find out what I can about … The Crowd."

As he pours coffee into his cup, he points at an empty mug. "Grab some coffee?"

Without a response, I walk over and fix a cup. Eyeing doughnuts on another table, I have to ask. "Can I get a doughnut, Staff?"

"They're for anyone who wants 'em, just leave a quarter."

All I have is a dollar. I leave it and take two doughnuts.

Checking out my clothes, Staff Sergeant Baylor says, "Your uniform's squared away, Green. Did it take you all night?"

I smile. "It took as long as needed, Staff Sergeant." The smile fades away. "Can I talk to you about my squad?"

"Sure, Corporal, what's on your mind?" He sits at his desk.

I move to the front of his desk, close to a folding chair left there from yesterday. I finish the last bite of my second doughnut. "There's no way I can force these men to shape up, Staff. That isn't going to happen unless I lead by example, and that starts today. I need to know all I can about these guys. How did they get to be The Crowd?"

Staff Sergeant Baylor takes a sip of coffee, looks up at me, then leans back. "It was about a year ago, around the time our pay started going south, when a corporal shows up. He seems to be squared away. He's black, has two years left on his contract, talks like he might want to make the Corps a career." Baylor sits straighter. "He's coming from Motor Transport Company. We had an opening in first squad." The staff sergeant takes a long pause. "I made him the squad leader. I actually thought this was the perfect match for an all-black squad. I couldn't have been more wrong. He

35

made them into The Crowd. He only lasted a few months." Baylor cups his hands around his coffee. "The guy ran with some gangs in Gary, tried to recruit Harris and a couple of the other Marines into that life. He got into trouble with the police, went AWOL, and we never saw him again. Sit, Green."

"Did any of the squad want to join those gangs?" I sit.

"You bet they did. I thought I was losing those Marines. We started to split the squad up, but it was Harris who kept them together and in line. Harris is a good Marine. He kept them from joining gangs and from becoming bad Marines. If only this pay bullshit wasn't happening, Harris would be corporal by now. But now he feels the Corps is screwing him over, and his pros and cons are suffering from it."

"Can I get a list of info on these guys? I need names, home addresses, stuff like that. I want to know as much as I can about them."

"Sure." Baylor gets up and strides to the filing cabinet behind Staff Sergeant Harden's desk. There he pulls out the file labeled "First Squad."

"I keep one of these on each squad in the platoon. Like you, Green, it's important for me to keep up to date on the Marines I'm responsible for." He pushes the cabinet drawer closed and turns to face me. "We didn't know what we were going to do with these men. Then you show up. Do you have a plan?"

"I do, Staff Sergeant. I want to keep it between me and the squad for the time being."

Baylor sits down with a look suggesting concern. I'm not sure if I overstepped the boundary of my rank. With the file grasped tightly in his hand, he says something I'm completely unprepared for.

"Green, I'm letting you in on a dirty little secret. You seem like you want to get through to these Marines. I feel we've done the right thing giving you first squad." He looks over my head, as if I'm sitting taller than I am, and hesitates. "What I'm about to tell you stays between you and me, understand?"

What the... "Yeah, Staff Sergeant, I understand."

"The Crowd, led by Harris, has stated they won't be going to the ATD this year if their pay is not straightened out. That doesn't sit well with the company commander. We can't have a mutiny in this company. They'll be court-martialed, made examples of."

I don't know what to say. I sit and wait for him to continue.

"We're counting on you to get them to change their minds. If they don't go, they'll be charged." He loosens his grip on the folder and hands it to me.

I open it and look inside, but I'm not reading anything. My mind is blank, waiting for him to say something.

"You're their last chance, Corporal."

I sit there and wonder how, on my second day back in the Marine Corps, the fate of nine Marines could lie in my hands. After everything I've been through. My marriage is falling apart, I lost my best friend, and now I'm told it's up to me to save these men from themselves. How do I get them to trust a white guy they don't know?

Oh, Bubba, I sure wish I could talk to you now, buddy. Wish I had you here. What do I do now?

CHAPTER 7

WINNING THEM OVER

BUBBA'S NOT HERE TO HELP me. No one is.
These Marines will be court-martialed if I can't get them to change their minds about the ATD.

All I know about them is what they call themselves, The Crowd. It defines them as something outside the Marine Corps. They've rebelled against every NCO assigned to take charge of them.

If I'm going to change their minds about the upcoming ATD, then I'll need to do it in two and a half drill weekends, five days.

I tell Baylor, "I want to take this squad and get to know them. Take them somewhere we can be alone. Do I have your permission?"

Staff Sergeant Baylor stares at me for a second. "The only thing they'd be missing is useless PM on vehicles that won't ever run, anyway. Okay, Corporal. You can have them. Make sure you stay busy. I don't want some officer to catch you goofing off. Got it?"

"Got it, Staff Sergeant."

Staff Sergeant Harden enters the office with some I & I Marines. We sit and talk until it's time for formation. I put the notepad in my side pocket and head down to where the company forms up. While waiting for the squad to fall in, I take a list of names from my pocket. I had put it together by rank and time in grade. First on the list is Lance Corporal Harris, followed by James and Gibson. Next are PFCs Clement, Wilson, Freeman, Wills, Cole, and Stokes.

The squad arrives while I'm looking it over.

Shit, I know their names, but I don't know their faces.

The men say nothing as, one by one, they fall in. I'm ignored.

Harris arrives next to me.

Okay, they're all here. Let's see how this goes.

I hand Harris the list of squad names. "Have the squad fall in, in this order."

He takes the list, studies it, and hands it back. "They're already in this order, Corporal." I wanted to get the squad in line with my list so I would know who was who. I never thought they would fall in while in proper rank order. That's a blunder I won't repeat.

Once the company forms, Staff Sergeant Baylor calls us to attention. The CO comes forward and announces the plan of attack for the day and dismisses the company. I move to the front of the squad and notice their uniforms are more squared-away than I expected. Maybe things won't be as bad as I was led to believe.

"Lance Corporal Harris, have the squad fall in somewhere no heavies can find us. I'll follow you."

Harris seems puzzled. "I'm not sure I understand what you mean."

"I want to have some private time with the squad. Somewhere we won't be found. Do you know of any place on this reserve center fitting that description?"

He shrugs. "What the hell, sure. Let's go, y'all. We're taking the day off."

The squad rambles over to a back section of the compound, where huge boulders sit on wide patches of grass. The site overlooks Lake Michigan. The cyclone fence surrounding the center keeps us from getting nearer to the beach. This area is exactly what I want, hidden and relaxing.

Each man finds a spot to sit. Some perch on large boulders, others on the grass. As I walk up from behind, Harris says, "You gonna tell Staff Sergeant Baylor where we go to hide, Green?"

"We're not hiding, Lance Corporal. We're having a class."

"This ain't a classroom. I don't see any desks," someone from the squad mumbles.

"What's your name, Private?"

"James. I'm not a private. I'm a lance corporal. Just like Harris."

"Where's your chevrons?" I ask.

James lights up a cigarette, and others in the squad follow his lead, something disciplined Marines would not do without permission from a senior NCO. I have lots to do to improve this squad and not a lot of time to do it.

"I don't have any lance corporal chevrons because Supply says they don't have another set."

I jot down his name and what he tells me. "We'll talk to Supply. Anybody else have a problem with Supply?"

A small Marine sitting on the highest boulder says, "I checked into Supply three months ago. I asked for an extra-small cover. Even gave them the paperwork from Schools Battalion to get one. I keep going back, and they keep telling me the same thing, we don't have anything. It's bullshit."

"It is bullshit. What's your name, Marine?"

"PFC Clement."

Another note and I move on.

Harris asks, "What are you doing, Green?"

"Lance Corporal, I'm your squad leader, and as your squad leader, there are things I need to address. It's my job." I stare at the giant of a man. "I'll always give you respect, Lance Corporal, by referring to you by your rank. You've earned it. I, too, have earned my rank and deserve equal respect." I scan the squad and wait to see if they get what I'm saying.

"Okay, Corporal Green." Harris joins the squad sitting on the boulders, and he seems to relax.

"Is there anybody else who has a problem with Supply?" No one comes forward, so I move on.

"I understand you guys have not been paid for some time. Lance Corporal Harris, it's been a year for you, hasn't it?"

"I don't know, maybe. I got a check last month for sixty-eight dollars. That's, like, almost a whole drill, so I don't know anymore."

PFC Willis laughs. "Do you think you're going to fix our pay problems? You ain't nothing but a corporal." The whole squad follows his lead and snickers.

Harris yells, "Knock it off!"

"No, I can't fix your pay. But you have a right to find out how much the Marine Corps owes you. Do any of you know how much that is? Do any of you know how far in arrears your pay goes?"

No one replies.

PFC Freeman speaks out. "What difference would that make?"

Harris answers, "At least you would know, dumb ass. Then the big weenie can't screw you."

Lance Corporal James shouts, "Yeah, that's right. We can know what they owe us. You're right on, Corporal."

Soon the whole squad is joining in. They start talking, with each one wondering how far they're behind and how much they're owed.

"Hey, Corporal," Cole yells, "you think we'll ever see that money?"

"Yes, PFC, you will." My plan is working. They're coming together under my leadership. I'll lead them to Supply and Payroll and fight for their rights. Together, as a force and as a team, we'll become a Marine Corps squad.

"The first thing we do is go to Supply, but we can't go looking like a mob. If some heavy sees us, we'll get stopped. Corporal Harris, put the squad into two fire teams and march them over in two columns. I'll follow."

Harris doesn't argue. He takes the squad and separates them, and we march to Supply. We pass the window of the maintenance building where I saw these men for the first time yesterday. Staff Sergeant Baylor is looking down, and I can see his amazement as he watches first squad march by.

Inside the building, the squad waits along the bulkhead as I head up the stairs to the office. Supply isn't going to give me anything without the proper paperwork. I'm going to have to bluff my way through. Our first sergeant's name is Stalker, a great name for a first sergeant.

I enter the office and approach Staff Sergeant Baylor. "Staff, can I have a file folder?" Then I ask Staff Sergeant Harden for a few sheets of supply request forms. "I'll bring them right back."

"What do you need them for?" Harden asks.

"I'd rather not say. I need to get something from Supply for my squad."

He hands me the official forms and says, "When you're done, destroy them. You never got them from me."

I grab a pen and fill in some gobbledygook to make it appear that something official is written on the forms. Then I put them in the folder.

Once we're all at Supply, I see the same Marine who checked me in. "Hey there, Lance Corporal. We need to talk."

"What is it, Corporal?"

With the squad behind me, I open the folder. The lance corporal can see the form is real and there's something written on it. Now I need to talk my way through this bluff. "Staff Sergeant Baylor sent me down here with these men. He contacted First Sergeant Stalker." My eyes move upward, making contact with his. "You know who that is?"

He nods.

"It seems these two Marines"—I motion for them to step forward—"Private First Class Cole and Lance Corporal James, have applied for"—I look down at the gobbledygook as if I'm reading off the paper—"an extra-small cover and lance corporal chevrons. You told then none are available. Are those items available now? If not, the first sergeant says he'll come down and find them himself."

The lance corporal stares for a moment then turns and goes to a back room where all the supply goods are. He returns shortly with a set of lance corporal chevrons and the extra-small cover. "The Marines are with me now. Do you want them to sign anything?"

"No, I'll take care of it." And we're gone.

Outside, the squad's laughter grows. They've never seen anything like this before. I tell them to keep this between us.

"It's almost time for chow and formation. We'll do pay right after."

"You'll like chow on Sunday, Corporal." PFC Willis shows a wide grin. "It's a hot meal catered in. Last month we had baked chicken, and it was good." His smile is evidence of his day so far.

The squad seems to be accepting me, though I know I still have a way to go. I'm hoping we're not shot down when we show up at Payroll.

Lunch is good. The squad all sits together, enjoying a meal of ham and sweet potatoes. I'm there as well but have little conversation with anyone. I'm not looking for friendship. I'm trying to gain trust and respect.

Chow and formation over, we move out of the mess hall. Headquarters is our destination. I tell the men to wait in an empty, partitioned office space. I close in on the payroll clerk. To my surprise, I'm instructed to have each Marine fill out a form and return it to the clerk. Facing only my men, I grin wide as I take the forms back to the squad. As a team, we complete the paperwork then return it to the clerk.

With Marine Corps professionalism, the clerk offers good news. "The information you're requesting should be available by next drill weekend."

The men seem skeptical about anything getting resolved. I attempt to reassure them. "I know you're thinking this is all bullshit and nothing is going to happen. I'll be down every Wednesday, that's my day off, and I'll do this until I get your information. Or they boot my ass out."

I face Harris. "Formation will be going at 1600 hours. We still have about two hours left. Let's find an empty trailer. I want to talk to the squad, and I don't want anyone to overhear what I'm going to say."

"Copy that, Corporal."

Inside one of the empty trailers filled with desks and a blackboard, the squad sits silently. I stand in front and get right to the point.

"I've heard some of you might not show up for the ATD this year because of your pay situation." Some grumbles come, but I continue. "I can understand your frustration. Let me ask you something. Anyone here ever get a tax refund?"

Almost everyone's hands go up.

"If you ever worked a job, paid taxes, then you filed taxes. And you probably received something back. Whether large or small, it was a check you could cash, and you knew the money was good."

"I sure did. Last year I got seven hundred bucks back," Gibson shouts.

"Shut up, man," Stokes says.

"One thing you can count on from the US Government, you will get paid, sooner or later. If any of you don't show up for your ATD, you'll lose all that back pay you're owed. If you show up, then somewhere down the line, just like your tax return, a big check is coming your way."

I let that settle in as each Marine appears to be giving it some thought. "Don't blow your money and your future because of some stupid ass jerkoff's mistake back in Kansas City. Once the pay is fixed, and it will be fixed, you'll wish you'd never made that decision. You're all grown men making up your own mind. You have plenty of time to change it before August. I hope you do."

"Where'd you hear this, Corporal?" Lance Corporal James asks. "This was a private letter we all signed to the CO."

"I can't reveal where. I gave my word, and I keep it. If anyone wants to change their mind, be here for the ATD."

The time is 1530. "Next drill, I'd appreciate shined boots with ironed uniforms. Let's look like squared-away Marines."

PFC Cole responds, "Copy that, Corporal Green."

CHAPTER 8

TIME TO LEAD

2 August 1980

IT'S 0400. THE TWO-WEEK ANNUAL training duty begins today. On the way down to the reserve center, Peggy and I are silent. We had an argument last night about the things we always fight about—her job, her cheating. The problems in our marriage steadily worsen. She doesn't want to be doing this drop-off, especially so early. But if she wants the car, she has no choice. In front of the headquarters building, I exit. There's no goodbye. I grab my pack and duffel bag from the back seat, close the door, and walk away.

A cool morning breeze, unusual for August, blows through the dark morning and chills me. I carry my pack and duffel bag over to the staging area for Motor Transport Platoon. As I set them down, I hear Baylor yell, "Corporal Green."

"Yes, Staff Sergeant."

"Are you going to have a squad this morning?"

Showing confidence while hiding my worry, I say, "Yes, Staff Sergeant, I am."

First squad finally received information about their pay last month. I hope that helps them make up their minds for this ATD. Even though the data's a month late, each man now knows how much back pay he's owed. Still, no one from the squad is here.

Most of the men, except for Harris, haven't been on an ATD. At last month's final formation, I explained what to expect and clarified what they will need to bring with them. I also wanted to give the men an extra incentive to show up, so I emphasized civilian clothes.

"We should get a day or two of liberty while we're down there," I explained. "That's not a guarantee, but be prepared."

It's 0500, and the buses are arriving. Most of the company is on deck. First squad ranks are still empty as the other squads in the platoon are all but complete. Staff Sergeant Baylor calls the platoon to fall in for roll call. I take my position at the head of an empty squad. Then PFC Clement falls in. He places his duffel bag down in front of his feet, turns, and smiles. I don't return the smile but only nod to acknowledge his presence. Moments later, Lance Corporal James falls in.

I lean over and ask James, "Where's Harris?"

Behind me I hear, "Don't worry, Corporal. I'm here."

One by one, each Marine falls in. Staff Sergeant Baylor notices my squad assembled and smiles. At 0530 I report, "All present and accounted for."

The order is given. "Motor Transport, fall out."

The buses fill with each platoon until the company is all on board. Our next stop is Marine Corps Base Camp Lejeune.

The weather in North Carolina is brutal in August. The average temperature is ninety degrees, but this first week, we've been closer to a hundred every day. The lack of supplies in the Marine Corps extends to the active side of the house as well. Motor T, assigned to Truck Company, is given only three vehicles to train with.

Staff Sergeant Baylor does his best to give as many drivers as he can a chance to train. For most, their days consist of performing vehicle preventive maintenance.

While attached to Truck Company, I take the written and driving tests I need to get my military license. Staff Sergeant Baylor made sure this would happen. In my record book, I receive the MOS rating of 3531, Motor Vehicle Operator. My goal is 3533, Tractor-Trailer Operator.

Thursday night rolls around, and everyone's excited about liberty over the weekend. But first we must pass a field day on Friday. Every nook and cranny in our sleeping quarters will be inspected. I'm talking everything from the windows and sills to the floors and walls. From our racks made perfectly to the heads we piss, shit, and shower in.

But that won't be the hardest part of this field day. The hardest part will be pleasing the inspectors, who won't be from the reserve side of the house but the regular side. On the first day I was here, I overheard two NCOs talking about how the reserve Marines don't even know how to do a simple PM. I can't help believing the regulars don't think much of us. Many of them may not even consider us real Marines. The inspection we receive may not be fair.

At Friday morning formation, our CO tells the company, "Today will be a different day of training. Instead of your normal schedule, you'll perform land navigation drills. Each platoon will do one drill shared by each of its squads. The team that completes the course and finds their flag in the fastest time will be excused and go immediately on liberty. The other squads will complete the field day. The courses are already laid out. Ten-hut. First Sergeant"— the first sergeant walks forward and faces the CO—"Take charge of the company."

"Aye, aye, sir." He salutes.

After an about-face, the first sergeant gets down to details. "At ease. Each squad from each platoon will receive a different starting time. There will be one flag for each squad to locate. Follow your compass to the different points on the map and then bring the flag back to the barracks. Get it done. Company ... A-ten-hut ... dismissed."

The squad looks depressed, so I ask, "What's wrong?"

Clearly discouraged, PFC Wilson says, "Hell, Corporal, we don't know anything about reading a compass or maps."

I look at Harris and glance across the squad. "Is that right? You people don't know how to use a compass?"

Harris shakes his head.

"Listen. When I was in 'Nam…" I watch their eyes light up, because until now, I don't think any of them knew I was a Vietnam vet. "I once had to call in an eight-digit grid without knowing where I was. I don't know how good these other squad leaders are, but I can still read a map and a compass. We have a chance to win this, and along the way, you people will learn how to use that compass and map."

PFC Cole asks, "You were in Vietnam?"

"Yeah, PFC, I was."

PFC Freeman asks, "How the hell old are you, Corporal?"

I ignore the question and accept our compass and map. Sergeant Morales, a Marine I & I who accompanied us from Gary, will coordinate the start of the drills.

He tells us, "Get in the truck. I'll drive you to your starting point. Once you kick off, your time will begin. Remember, bring the flag back to the barracks, not where you start. Any questions?"

"How much time between each squad?" I ask.

"Fifteen minutes. Anything else?"

I shake my head. We get in, and he drops us off about ten minutes down the road. He checks his watch for the time to start, and at 0800 we begin.

The map is simple, and along the way, I show the squad the basics of reading a map and using a compass. I have no problem following this map, but I need an advantage to win. Camp Lejeune is full of swamps, high grass, trees, and flat areas. After discovering coordinates circled on the bottom of our map, I plot them and believe that is where our flag will be. For safety, instructors always mark the coordinates to the halfway point on the bottom of these maps. Then in case of an emergency, we can use them as a point of reference.

"Harris, look at this."

Harris looks where I'm pointing. "So?"

"You know what? That's where the flag is. If I'm right, we can knock off a lot of time by forgetting these directions and going straight to it. I want to give it a try."

"If you're wrong, we're screwed."

I remember my team leaders from Vietnam. When we were in the bush, if they had a feeling, no matter what anyone said, they went with their gut. "I know I'm right."

I get the squad moving. We're off the regular course by going our own way. About thirty minutes later and more than halfway to the coordinates, we come to a stream ten feet wide. The water is brown, and twigs, leaves, and debris are floating in it. The current is hardly moving.

"Okay, we have to cross this," I tell the squad.

"Forget that shit," Gibson says. "There are snakes in that water."

"No, there aren't," I insist.

James protests. "This is North Carolina. They have rattlers and water moccasins. You're crazy, Corporal. I ain't going in that water."

I look to Harris for help, but he says nothing. The big man looks scared.

How am I going to get them to cross?

I'm sure the stream is clear of snakes. At least, I hope so. The only way to get them into the water is to show them it's safe.

I look at Harris, shake my head, and walk into the middle of the stream. The water is dirty and cold but only knee-deep. I turn to see them standing there, staring at me as if I'm nuts. "Okay, Marines, it's safe. Let's go so we can win this." Still, they don't move. I raise my voice. "What the hell? Lance Corporal Harris, get those men across."

"I don't think so, Corporal." Harris points at a stick making a wave in the current. "Look there. It's a snake."

I rant. "What a bunch of shit. You people wouldn't last one day in 'Nam." I slosh over, pull the stick out, and hold it in the air. "Is this your snake, Lance Corporal?" I fling it to the shore and offer my hand as a gesture to assist. Insulted, Harris gets angry. He storms across the stream with James on his heels. All the Marines follow, and we're on our way again.

We find our flag at the coordinates circled on the map and return it in record time. The sergeant who dropped us off seems to think we somehow cheated. I tell him, "I gambled and went off your game plan and formed my own."

"How did you know where to look for the flag?" he asks.

Smiling, I answer, "Just lucky, I guess."

"Hmm," he says. "How much compass training have you had?"

"Enough to get me through 'Nam."

"You're a Vietnam vet? I should have known."

At noon formation, Staff Sergeant Baylor announces first squad is the winner.

The pride in first squad shines for the first time since I've known them. For a long while, they've been the outsiders, the unit known as The Crowd. Now they're the squad that won the compass course. They're the best in the platoon. They go on liberty while the rest stay behind to clean the barracks.

"Liberty will run from fifteen hundred hours today until eighteen hundred hours Sunday. Staying in town overnight is strongly discouraged," Baylor warns. "If you get into trouble, being a reservist will not keep you from a court-martial under UCMJ."

Eager for showers, the squad heads straight to the barracks before they're closed for the field day. I join them in the head, but I'm unsure if I will be welcome to tag along or if I should even consider it. I'm their squad leader, and as such, I have to be careful I don't cross a line. Marine Corps regulations that govern partying with the troops are serious, though I'm not sure they apply to an E-4.

I'm getting dressed in my civvies when Harris walks over to my rack. "Hey, Corporal Green, you hang with ... The Crowd?"

"About that name, Harris. Don't you think it's time...?"

"I know, Corporal, it's time to be Marines. You won't hear it from me again."

I look at the big man, questioning his sincerity. Harris smiles. "So you coming, or what?"

"You're damn right I'm coming. Let's tear this town up."

We head down to the company office. On our way, we pass other barracks where Marines are beginning their field days. PFC Stokes asks, "Hey, Corporal, we pulled it off, didn't we?"

"Yeah, we did."

Freeman says, "Shit, y'all. That was all Corporal Green."

With liberty passes in hand, at 1500 we call two taxis and head out to Jacksonville. We're quite a sight, even for 1980. Nine very tall and very black young men and one white guy, out on the town together. We hit all the bars, from disco to hard rock. The biggest joke that night is when we walk into a blues bar filled with black people. As the only white guy, I'm feeling a little nervous. Harris reassures me, "Ain't nothing to be nervous about, Corporal. We got your back."

The blues bar is the quietest place we've been in. The squad ignores a three-piece blues band and tries to get me to tell some war stories. PFC Freeman says, "Hey, Harris, ax Corporal Green to tell us some Vietnam stories. He'll do it for you." He does, and I do.

"We're pinned down in that damn rice paddy, surrounded, and darkness was approaching. If we didn't get out before nightfall, we were dead." The whole squad is glued to every word I say. "From the east, I see this lone CH-46 with its tail high in the air, hauling ass—"

"You boys need a refill?" a waitress interrupts.

"Yes, ma'am. On me." Slipping her a twenty-dollar bill, I say, "Keep the change."

As she leaves for more beers, Stokes asks, "What happened then, Green?"

I finish my story, exciting them with the tale of how we got out but keeping to myself the part about the Marine killed in action.

Not wishing to share any more combat stories with them, I talk about the time on Dong Den that Rock Apes attacked the OP.

"Chief and I moved to the other side of the LZ because he had to shit, and the rule was, no one goes across the LZ alone after dark. I stood there while he was shitting and gazed into a black night, no visibility. My rifle was resting on my magazine pouch when I heard something in the wire. I called Chief, asking if he heard anything."

The waitress brings our beers, and I stop to take a drink. With his eyes open wide, PFC Freeman pleads, "Come on, Corporal. What y'all do?"

The story goes on, and I tell them how the whole team was on alert. When I get to the part where Chief and I found out they were apes, they all laugh. I share more stories, but certain memories, I keep to myself. Those were just for Bubba and me. Maybe someday I'll talk about them, but not today.

To make sure nobody gets into trouble, I stay sober, watching over my squad. We head back and walk into the barracks at 0300. The Marines who stayed behind to complete the field day are asleep. Their liberty will start in the morning. First squad will be sleeping in.

CHAPTER 9

MOVING ON

7 August 1982

THE LAST TWO YEARS IN the Corps have seen quite a turnaround with the unit and in the reserve center itself. Payroll finally got its act together and fixed everyone's pay last year. First squad got their back pay as I told them they would. Gibson used his money to get married, and Freeman bought a new car. First squad's decision to go on the ATD in 1980 proved to be the right one for each of them.

I left the squad in January 1982 to become the company embarkation NCO. Harris received his promotion to corporal that same month and took over as squad leader. He left the Corps with an honorable discharge in April of '82. I came back to the squad after Corporal Harris left the unit.

Most of the Marines from first squad are all discharged now, and the only one left is Lance Corporal Clement. The small Marine I first met sitting on top of a boulder is now the only member from the original squad of 1980. He started taking MCI courses and applied for NCO school. When he graduated number one, he received a meritorious promotion to corporal. With a year left on his contract, he's my number two. He may be small in stature, but he stands tall in the Marine Corps. He's giving serious consideration to reenlisting. Ooh Rah!

The reserve center has had a complete makeover. The fire damage I first noticed the day I checked in is gone. A new headquarters building now stands in its place, and it's state of the art. It's two stories with offices for all those in command and many classrooms for the troops training. Since the completion of the building, the mobile trailers are gone. Today, along with the Motor T garage, Heavy Equipment Platoon has theirs as well. Both the Water Platoon and the electricians have structures now.

Staff Sergeant Baylor received a promotion to gunnery sergeant in May. Later we picked up an officer, Captain Moralie, who assumed the role of platoon commander. The captain is a tall man, six foot three, and he'll demand no less of himself than what he demands from his Marines. That's how he runs his platoon.

His first day was on a June drill weekend. He told us back then he'd been in motor transport his entire Marine Corps career. He mentioned how he completed his regular contract after serving twelve years. He decided to continue in the reserves until he reaches twenty years.

I remember when he said, "The problems of the past will stay in the past. The trouble with pay and old equipment is over. We're now supplied with the most updated equipment the Corps has. Our mechanics are being stocked with parts for our vehicles. As soon as all our trucks are roadworthy, we'll be heading out on convoys."

The men stood at ease and smiled when they heard that. I smiled too. The thought of going on a convoy to train is what we had all been waiting for. I believed this new leader would take us there.

Later that day, Captain Moralie called me into his office. The captain's door was open, and I saw he had wasted no time in preparing his new space. A picture of a woman and two children—his family, I assume—sat on a plain green metal desk. I knocked on a side panel. He looked up and waved me in, and I noticed my record book on the corner of his desk.

He said I had a four-point-nine on my proficiency and conduct, Pro and Cons, over the last two quarters. And he reported I had nothing lower than a four-point-seven. With more than twenty-four months' time in grade, I'd get my promotion soon.

He tells me, "Gunny Baylor has recommended you for platoon sergeant. Though you're only a corporal, I concur." Pausing for a moment, he asks, "Do you understand the responsibilities of the platoon sergeant?"

"Yes, sir. My first responsibility is to assist and to take over in the event Gunny Baylor is unable to perform his duties. To perform platoon operations and ensure our combat readiness. And finally, to maintain our capabilities to deploy if activated."

I must have gotten it right, because he said, "I'll announce the change at platoon formation."

I became platoon sergeant later that day.

4 September 1982

Captain is keeping his word. It's Saturday morning, and September drill weekend is about to begin. Motor T Platoon is preparing to leave the drill center on the first convoy in a long time.

I arrive at 0400 to get everything ready. Setting up the convoy is the job of the platoon sergeant. I volunteer a few of my men to join me—they weren't happy, but that's life in the Marine Corps.

Lined up and ready to go as soon as morning formation concludes are seven M-35 two-and-a-half-ton six-by-six trucks, one M939 five-ton wrecker truck, and a ten-ton semi with a D75 bulldozer loaded on the low-boy trailer. There are two updated jeeps. The one in front of the convoy is for the commander, and the one at the rear is for the second in command, most likely someone from the I & I staff. I'll be in the middle, driving the ten-ton tractor-trailer.

Last month, Staff Sergeant Harden gave me the driving and written test for the 3533 MOS, Logistics Vehicle System Operator, or ten-ton tractor-trailer driver. I passed, and the CO signed them into my record book. The convoy's destination today will be our sister company, Sixth Engineers Support Battalion, Alpha company, located in South Bend, Indiana. The trip is short, only sixty-five miles one way. We'll have lunch and head back.

3 October 1982

It's drill weekend. I show up at 0500 and walk into the company office. A clerk in charge of records walks up to me as I'm pouring myself a cup of coffee.

"Congratulations, Green."

I smile but have no idea what he means.

He looks at me. "You don't know what I'm talking about, do you?"

"No. What?"

"You're promoted. First of October. Congratulations."

Almost dropping my coffee, I reply, "You fucking with me?"

"No, the warrant came down last week. Something about your MOS got you promoted."

Still not believing this news, I find Captain Moralie in his office. "Captain, the clerk says I'm being promoted to sergeant?"

While looking through his desk drawers, he answers, "That's what I've been told, Corporal. It seems your new MOS has open slots for sergeant, and you qualify with time in service and time in grade." He pauses and looks at me. "You were on the top of the list. Are you squared away?" He smiles. "Yeah. You're always squared away. Get your corporal chevrons off when you go to formation this morning. The CO will call you up and present your promotion warrant."

"Copy that, sir." *Holy shit, I'm a sergeant.*

My Marine Corps career is moving along great. I'm promoted to sergeant, I'm driving the tractor-trailer, and I'm Motor Transport Platoon sergeant.

The MCI classes I took have taught me a lot about convoy maneuvers. That, along with my own personal experience in combat, will help me train these men. Books are important, but firsthand experience is always better.

Over at the American Legion, I find Vietnam and Korean War veterans. These men are extremely helpful. I pick their brains to find out what it was like to run convoys in combat. I listen to their stories of ambushes and booby traps. I learn what works and what's bullshit. All this, I pass on to my men. I drill it into them until they know it like they know the backs of their hands.

We're not at war, but I know if war comes, it will come without warning. It's my job to make sure they have the training to come back alive.

My civilian employment has gotten a whole lot better in 1982. I'm now working for one of the top bread companies in the country and making good money. My route centers around a place called Crown Point, a small town in Northwest Indiana where the sales are always good.

I wish my marriage could go as well. Things did get better for a while. Peg's staying out late at night stopped after she admitted she'd been cheating. Our marriage started looking like we were going to make it until we bought the new house in Hessville.

In the spring of 1982, Peg and I made a move we hoped would help our marriage. We purchased a house that was more than we could afford on my income alone. We figured that by keeping the house in Hammond and renting it out, we'd have additional income. Peg would also look for a job at the nearby Kroger grocery store, and we could make a go of it.

The new house was huge. It had four bedrooms, one for each of our children. With a two-and-a-half-car garage and a full basement, it was the perfect home.

Everything was fine for the first two months. Then Peg told me she got laid off from Kroger. When she said she'd talked with Janice and would get her old job back, I felt sick to my stomach.

Suspicious, I called Kroger. They couldn't give me any information, but later I found out Peg had lied about being laid off.

By July, Peg was staying out late again. At first, it was only until two in the morning. But on days when I didn't have to use the car to go to work, she came in as late as four.

During this time, I was home alone and had become anxious and restless. I knew what she was doing, and I couldn't sleep and would lie awake at night. I got angry and started to take it out on the kids. Sometimes I hated her, and sometimes I wanted to leave. I felt so alone.

As the cheating went on, I began to get jealous that I was home while she was out having a good time. She wouldn't admit it, but I knew she was cheating. I had to fight the temptation to do the same thing. I'd ask myself, Could I cheat? Is it okay for me if I know she's cheating?

It's a cold midmorning in November 1982. I'm inside the doorway of a grocery store in Crown Point, Indiana. I've already been waiting for more than ten minutes to get my bread products checked in but still have three vendors ahead of me. I'm thinking this is going to take another twenty minutes.

"Either step out or get inside, but close that door," the clerk shouts.

I step all the way in and close the door.

Damn, this is ridiculous. Sometimes it takes forever to get checked in here.

A soft voice from behind me asks, "You want to get checked in?"

I turn, and there's the most beautiful blond-haired, blue-eyed woman I've ever seen. "Yeah, sure." I hand her my paperwork and stare. "You're new here? Don't remember seeing you before."

"Not new. Been here a while, but I usually work in the store. I've seen you before. My name's Cindy."

"Hi, I'm Rick."

"I know." She smiles.

Surprised by her answer, I stand and continue to stare at her lovely blue eyes. Her face lights up with a smile that seems to invite me to smile back. Her skin shines, its soft glow begging to be caressed.

"You ready to begin?" she asks.

I stutter, "Oh, yeah, sure." While we check off each bread product, I interrupt, attempting to get to know her. "This weekend, I'm going to a ball."

"A ball, really?"

"Yeah. The Marine Corps celebrates its birthday every year on November tenth. We're holding our annual ball in celebration of that event this year on Saturday, November sixth. We're going to be right here in Crown Point, at the Serbian Hall, next to the American Legion. You know where that is?"

"You're a Marine?"

"Yes, I am. I'm a sergeant in the United States Marine Corps. There'll be about two hundred and fifty of us. Everyone will be in their dress blue uniforms, and there'll be dinner and dancing."

"A real ball? I'd love to see that."

I wish I could invite you to be my date.

"The Marine Corps is the toughest branch of service in America," she tells me.

"You're right. How do you know that?"

"My dad was a Navy Seabee during World War II and served with the Marines. He says they're tough."

"Your dad sounds like somebody I'd like to meet."

"You're all checked in. You coming back tomorrow?"

"Sure. Are you working tomorrow?"

"Yes, I'll try to check you in again, if you want. If I do, you'll get out of here faster."

"Sounds great."

Man, I want to see her again.

CHAPTER 10

SOMETIMES LIFE IS ALL IT GIVES YOU

21 February 1983

I T'S TWO IN THE MORNING when I wake to find Peggy still isn't home. She promised her cheating would end and there would be no more of these nights. For a while, she kept her word. But now her actions show me that she wants to be single. It hurts, but it's time I deal with it.

I don't want to pick up the phone and call the store when I know the answer will be like every other time. "Peggy is busy in the back room, checking the stock, and will call you as soon as she can." Of course, that call will never come.

I know our marriage is ending, but deep inside, I wish it would work. Against my own better judgment, I dial the number and listen to it ring.

"Hello."

"Hello, Michelle. Where's Peggy?"

She hesitates. I can tell Michelle doesn't want to be in the middle.

"Peggy's stocking in the back room. Let me get her." Two minutes later, she comes back with the standard answer. "She's busy."

I say nothing. There's dead silence.

"Rick, are you still there?"

Angry, I'm almost shouting. "Yes, I'm here. I want to know where Peg is, and you're going to tell me."

In an instant, Michelle breaks down. "I'm so sorry. I can't lie anymore. Janice and Peggy took off about eight o'clock and told me if you call, to tell you 'I'm busy' and to keep making excuses. What she's doing is wrong."

"Please, this isn't your fault. If they come back before you close tonight, don't say anything about talking to me. I'll take care of everything. One thing, do you know where it is they like to go?"

"A place called Manny's in Munster. That's all I know. I'm so sorry."

"Thank you, Michelle. Now forget we ever talked. Good night."

Peggy always takes the car to work, making it impossible for me to check up on her. Besides, I can't leave the kids here alone, so she feels sure I won't catch her doing anything wrong. But I have a plan I hope will get the truth from her.

A couple of hours later, Peggy pulls into our driveway. She walks through the door and up the stairs into the darkened living room. She's surprised when she spots the glow from my cigarette. I draw in and then exhale a plume of smoke, filling the air above me. "I've been waiting for you, Peg."

"You startled me." She appears panicked. "Is there something wrong with one of the kids?"

"The kids are fine. We're not."

"What are you talking about? I'm sorry I had to work so late. We had a late truck delivery and—"

"Stop. Just stop!" I inhale another puff from my cigarette and lean over to turn on a lamp next to my chair. Both of us squint from the brightness. "I know where you were tonight."

"I was at work. Where do you think I was?"

"I asked our neighbor to watch the kids, and I called a taxi. I went to the store. It was nine o'clock. Both you and Janice were gone."

Peggy looks shocked, but she's ready, almost as if she's rehearsed her response to this exact situation. "Janice had to get some special supplies from some guy, and it made her nervous to go alone. She asked me to come with her, that's all."

I shake my head and exhale. "I had the taxi take me to a place called Manny's. Ever hear of it?" I pause as she takes that in. "It's a great place. You and Janice might want to give it a shot. Oh, wait, you already did." I let that simmer for a moment as I watch her expression turn worrisome. "I saw you two there. I saw who you were with. Do you ever tell those guys you're married?"

That's all it takes. She starts to cry and moves to the edge of the sofa across from me. She fumbles while trying to light a cigarette. "I suppose you want to hear all the details?"

"I want to hear the truth."

Peg picks up an ashtray from the end table next to her, leans back in the sofa, and lets loose a big exhale of smoke. Wiping tears from her eyes, she asks, "Where should I begin?"

"It's always best to start at the beginning."

After a smirk, she does. The more details she reveals, the more I'm horrified and appalled by the extent of her betrayal. Peggy seems relieved to finally admit what she's done. This secret life must be a terrible weight on her shoulders. After all I've been through these past few years—all those long, agonizing nights of wondering where my wife was, what she was doing, who she might be with—I still can't help pitying her.

She finishes, and a silence settles over the room. I look down the hallway, where my children lie sleeping in their rooms. I know what I'm about to say is going to affect them more than it will either of us, but this is something I must say. This cannot go on, and it cannot be fixed.

I whisper, as if I don't want anyone else to hear. "Peggy, I'm filing for divorce. There's no way we can stay together any longer."

I wait for a response, and like a guilty teenager, she lets her eyes go to the floor.

"There are two ways we can handle this," I say. "I get my own attorney and you get yours, or we get one attorney and he handles both our cases. That's the least expensive way to go. What do you think?"

Peg looks at me with sadness. "One attorney sounds good."

"It's best if we tell the kids together. Can we do it later today, after school?"

Peg nods.

It's hard to look into her sheepish gray face. I turn away while saying, "I'll be moving out this morning. I'll pick up the rest of my things when I come back this afternoon."

Peg won't look into my eyes either. "Oh yeah, we'll have to wait to tell the kids. Your daughter is staying over at her friend's tonight."

"Okay, tomorrow, then."

Peg follows me into our bedroom and watches me pack a bag. Stuffing shirts, underwear, and socks into a duffel, I break the silence. "I've got to get going. I'm already late for work. And I'll have to keep the car since I need it for my job. I'll try to arrange to get you a vehicle as soon as possible." She agrees.

As I leave, I see the sadness on her face. She stands in the bedroom doorway and pleads, "Maybe this can still work. Maybe … we can work." I begin to walk past when she touches my arm. Her chin trembles as she implores, "I don't want to throw fifteen years away."

I briefly hold my breath before I answer. Then, looking at her with an aching chest, I say, "You did that the moment you were with those men." I brush past her, heading for the door.

She calls out, "Rick, please. I'll be better."

My hand on the doorknob, I stop and look down, pausing for a few seconds. I turn the knob and walk out.

For the last fifteen years, Peggy and the children have been my life. Now, everything is changing.

The next day, I find a lawyer and file for divorce. That's when I learn Peggy has decided to drop out of the mutual-lawyer agreement and get her own attorney. I'll have to pay for both. That's how it works under Indiana law.

Losing someone who's been part of me for so long is difficult, but having someone who cares for me can help take some of the sadness away. That person is Cindy.

I've known Cindy for several months, but we've never slept together. I expect that will change once Cindy finds out I have nowhere to go. Renters live in my other property, so I plan to live in a hotel.

When Cindy invites me to move in with her, I accept with a

smile. Our relationship moves fast, and I'm happier than I ever expected. Since the first day I met her, I dreamed of this. Now it's happening.

19 May 1984

It's our wedding day. We decorate the American Legion Hall in Crown Point with beautiful spring flowers. My family is here with Cindy's family. Her son and my three children, along with our friends, sit and wait for the ceremony to begin.

An arch filled with flowers stands where Cindy and I will take our vows. I wait there with the justice of the peace. Cindra Jo, the woman I call CJ, walks out a back door and toward me. She's wearing a beautiful white dress with vintage floral lace. The skirt reaches her ankles. My eyes fill with joy as I look upon the woman I'm about to marry. In front of our families, we say our own vows, then the party begins.

The woman I met that day in November of 1982 is a blessing. My divorce from Peg has been difficult, especially on Cindy. Peg tries to attack me everywhere, including a serious effort to turn our children against me. She threatens to go to court for more money. What she's doing has put a financial strain on Cindy and me. Through it all, Cindy has my back. As a little jab at Peggy's pride, my new wife writes and signs all the child support checks herself.

My son Kevin rebels against his mother. He doesn't want to live at her house. She admits he's too much for her to handle and allows me to have custody. Cindy immediately accepts him as a son, and Kevin accepts her as his mom. Cindy's son and Kevin are growing up as brothers, and that's a good thing. I know my daughters aren't being properly cared for, but I can't get a judge to move against Peg. They tell me, "Not enough evidence of serious harm."

Life in my home is great, but I wish it were like that for my girls.

CHAPTER 11

WHAT IS TO COME?

"WE'RE OVER THE DESERT, SIR." I look up, and a stewardess is standing above me. Out the airplane window, I see sand below. It appears to flow in slow motion like a calm brown ocean. Something moves past the wing, and I follow it upward until it disappears in the sunlight. Something else approaches, and as it does, a stream of smoke comes from the tail. Whatever that was, it strikes the engine, and an explosion rocks the aircraft back and forth. It begins to plummet. I turn to the Marines on board and see the fear in their eyes. The engine is burning as the plane lurches, continuing downward. My words drag as I yell out a warning. "We're going down!"

The desert sand suddenly erupts past my window, and the screams make me cover my ears with my hands. Fire is everywhere, and smoke begins to choke and blind all on board. The shrieking stops, and there's an eerie quiet. I turn and see the back section of the plane is gone, and so are most of my men. Even though the plane is filled with smoke and flames, the sun is shining through gaping holes in the plane. Women and children are walking around the aircraft, and I stare at this bizarre sight, devoid of thought.

I'm on the floor of the plane, slowly crawling to an open side and stopping when I feel something warm and wet. I look down and cringe at the sight of the lifeless, blood-covered body of the stewardess I was talking to moments before the rocket took us down. Her eyes are open wide, staring at nothing. My head throbs as I try to clear my eyes with the back of my hand. Suddenly I'm up and being helped out. "Come on, Staff Sergeant. We've got to go," the one helping me says.

Outside the plane, I'm kneeling down. I look around, and my men and small children are lying around the burning aircraft. Many aren't moving, either injured or dead. I stand and start issuing orders to the one who helped me out of the plane. "Find Doc. Help these people." I try to see who he is, but his face is a blur. As he moves away, I stop him. "Wait! Get weapons and ammo to the men."

Explosions are everywhere. The attack is relentless. My men are dying. Across the sand, the women and children are all dead.

One Marine yells out, "Staff Sergeant, there are too many. We can't stop them."

I scream, "We will! We have to!"

A bullet strikes my arm, and I look down in disbelief. Blood gushes out, covering my whole body. Another bullet burns my leg. The next one tears into my ribs, but I feel no pain. My eyes are open, but there's only darkness. Am I dead?

I'm walking down an endless corridor crowded with people all moving in the same direction. The dimensions of the passageway seem to change according to the number of people moving through. The ceiling is rounded, and while there's no visible lighting, plenty of light is available. There are no windows or doors, just smooth surfaces with small depressions every few feet.

Along the way, I see that everyone is walking alone. But there's someone—not like a friend or acquaintance but more like a guide—walking behind. This being seems to shine or glow—he or she; I'm not sure of the sex—but it doesn't matter. I would say this is some escort, and each person has his or her own, though when I look behind, I don't see mine.

I continue to walk, and though I can stop if I want, I don't. I keep moving, as if something extraordinary is waiting for me up ahead. Sometimes I see a person stop and stare at one of the depressions. I slow down to see what they're looking at, but there is nothing, yet the emotions on their faces tell me they're viewing something very personal. They laugh, cry, or clasp their hands together, praising God.

A voice from behind asks, "What are you looking for, Richard?"

I don't know until I'm asked. "My daughter is lost."

Taking my hand, my guide walks me down the hall and stops at a depression, saying, "This one is for you."

I stare as my escort glows so brightly it hurts my eyes. I turn away and look at the depression in the shiny wall. Suddenly I can see down to a mountain cave where my youngest daughter, Katie, is inside, sitting on a rock and crying, alone and lost. The family are all frantically looking for her. Cindy is also alone and looking desperate as she searches for our daughter.

I call to her, telling her where Katie is. Does she hear me? Cindy looks up. She shudders and then smiles. She heard me. Cindy yells, "This way. Katie's over here." She moves in the direction I told her, and soon Katie is found. The whole family embraces our little girl and each other with joy and relief. The images disappear.

I turn to ask my guide, "This is all I can see? Are they going to be okay? Will Katie be okay?" The guide smiles and disappears.

"Wake up, sir, and fasten your seat belt. We'll be landing soon," the stewardess says with a smile.

Waking with sweat on my brow and fear as real as any I've ever felt before, I ask, "We're here … in Hawaii?"

"Yes, sir. Are you all right? You look upset."

I try to smile. "Yes, I'm fine." Then sitting up straighter and a bit brighter, I respond, "How can I not be? I'm in Hawaii."

Her smile widens as she walks away.

I turn to my men behind me and am reminded of my dream, my nightmare. It was so real. I've never felt anything that real before, not from a dream. Man.

I'm glad there's no desert war in my future.

It's August 1987, and this ATD will be two weeks in Hawaii. Easy duty attached to a Seabee unit doing minor construction work.

I'm on an all-expenses-paid vacation to Hawaii, and I'm going to enjoy it!

I'm in charge of six Marines, and together we'll spend our free time on the beaches and explore Honolulu nightlife. We'll sightsee at Pearl Harbor, check out some volcanoes and famous waterfalls, and of course, attend a luau. I promised these guys all this. Why? The Marine Corps doesn't often send reservists to Hawaii for a two-week ATD. Such an opportunity just doesn't happen, and if it does, you take full advantage.

Our mission is to report every day to a Navy construction site. The best part, I found out, is that we will be on the same schedule as the Navy, so my Marines and I will start at 0900 and end no later than 1500, except on Friday. Those days end at 1400. We get a one-and-a-half-hour lunch thrown in as well, and our weekends are off. You gotta love the Navy.

My highlight will be a visit to HMM 364 Purple Foxes stationed here at Marine Corps Air Station Kaneohe Bay. Since becoming a staff sergeant, I'm not required to stay with the troops, though on most days, I will. I'll turn my Marines over to Navy Chief Petty Officer Jones, whose rank is E-7, one above mine. He'll be in charge of the work site. We talked on the phone, and he informs me my Marines will be putting together window – and doorframes and maybe laying a cement pad.

On the first day, I decide to drive over to the air station to visit the Purple Foxes. I want to share the story of how my recon team was saved that day in the rice paddies of Vietnam. When I arrive, I meet some of the pilots of today's CH-46s. I sit in the ready room with the young crews of these Purple Foxes and tell my story.

Then I get to the part about how our recon team was pinned down most of the day, and as night was approaching, a helicopter squadron took a mission to fly into our hot LZ and pull us out under heavy enemy fire. That chopper was HMM 364, Purple Foxes.

"I remember it like it happened yesterday. I was the radioman. I just got the word from Battalion that choppers were inbound for our position. I told the team, 'Purple Fox is coming in to get us.' That news brought hope to us all."

As I tell the story, they hang on every word.

"High above us, a lone CH-46 is flying in circles—"

"The chase bird," one of the crew listening blurts out.

"That's right. On the radio, I hear, 'Melody Time, this is Purple Fox. LZ report, over.' I give the report. Tell him where he'll most likely take fire and where we're located. I pop the smoke, but he doesn't respond. He already knows where we are. I spot him in the distance, down the rice paddies. His tail is high in the air, and he's moving fast."

"Had to be doing a hundred and fifty or more," another of the crew says.

"Yeah, I guess." I continue, "Two Cobra gunships pull in front of him, maybe a hundred yards ahead, one on his left and the other on his right." I use my hands to demonstrate what it looked like to us on the ground. "They were escorting him in."

"The Cobras fired into the tree line in front of the 46. Just as he gets to us, an enemy RPG lands right in front of him and explodes. Water and debris fly all over the cockpit. He rises high in the air, and I think he's leaving. I yell out but then realize he's turning the cockpit away from the trees and pointing his .50-caliber machine gun at the enemy, while directing the bird's tailgate toward us. As soon as he's on the ground, the crew chief runs out the back with a .60-caliber machine gun strapped to his shoulder. While laying down cover, he yells for us to get on board. We pick up our wounded and run for the chopper. All this time, the air cover is keeping the VC heads down with rockets, mini guns, and napalm. Once we're all on the bird, we take off. The fifties stop firing, and we clear our weapons. Our next stop was the Navy hospital at Da Nang."

I finally get the chance to thank the men of Purple Fox when I tell them, "Purple Fox saved our lives that day. We never—I never—

got the chance to tell the crew and the pilots thanks. I knew they didn't have to accept that mission, but they did. I can't tell them personally, so let me at least say thank you to you guys." I pause. "Thank you for saving my life that day in Vietnam."

This gives me the closure I never had until I got this opportunity to be with these Marines. There's nothing I'm more grateful for on this ATD than the visit to HMM 364 Purple Fox.

The ATD ends, and we board another jetliner back to Chicago then on to Indiana. The work we did in Hawaii had nothing to do with our jobs in the Corps, but it was easy, and we spent our time off doing things I never could have done anywhere else. I'll always remember the nightclub entertainment in downtown Honolulu and the sightseeing at Pearl Harbor, the beautiful waterfalls and the time we spent on the most breathtaking beaches I've ever seen. The only thing that could have made this better would be if Cindy were here with me.

20 July 1990

I'm sitting down watching television with Cindy when we hear about Saddam Hussein, the dictator of Iraq, threatening Kuwait over oil and money. The president has ordered some naval maneuvers in the Persian Gulf to warn this guy not to mess around.

Cindy asks, "What's that all about?"

"I don't know. I think it's from when Iraq was fighting Iran during the Carter or Reagan administrations. I guess Iraq owes money to Kuwait and someplace called the Arab Emirates. He doesn't think he has to pay it back."

With a wrinkled brow, she asks, "You think it could turn into a shooting war?"

"No, I really doubt it. Those kinds of things never go anywhere. This guy might be a little crazy, but he ain't stupid. Besides, if anything happens, it wouldn't involve the reserves. Don't worry, CJ. Don't worry."

CHAPTER 12

RUMORS OF WAR

2 August 1990

I'M DRIVING DOWN US 30 to make a delivery when the radio program I'm listening to is interrupted for a special report. "The Associated Press has just reported Saddam Hussein has ordered Iraqi forces into Kuwait."

Shit! He's the one Cindy and I were talking about a few weeks ago. What the hell.

All I can think about is whether this has the chance to turn into a big war for America. At first, I'm excited at the possibility of being called into service. The thought of performing my duties in a combat command role captivates me. Then the reality of war comes rushing back to mind, and I hope it never comes to pass.

I forgive myself for those first thoughts of excitement. I am, after all, a Marine, and the chance to do what I'm trained to do is always exhilarating. It's something every Marine wants to do. I know that many of my guys in the platoon would be excited to go off to war, the same as I was that first time.

I arrive home, and Cindy and the kids are glued to the television. "Have you heard, Dad?" my oldest son asks excitedly.

"You mean about Iraq invading Kuwait? Yeah, I heard."

"No. Not just that. President Bush is going to send in Marines to stop him from going any farther."

Two days later, it's reserve drill weekend. Motor Transport

Platoon no longer has an officer in charge. Captain Moralie left the unit six months ago. Gunny Baylor is the senior enlisted and the acting platoon commander. I picked up staff sergeant three years ago and replaced the gunny as Motor Transport chief. The company commander seems to think there's a chance, small as it may be, that we might be called into active duty if the First Marine Division goes to the Persian Gulf. The Corps depends heavily on certain units in the reserves to fulfill their needs. Sixth Engineers Battalion is one of them. I guess if the battalion goes, so does Support Company.

We're spending the weekend catching up on our wills and any last-minute paperwork required to go on active duty. I'm not taking word of what we did this weekend home to Cindy. The last thing I need is for her to worry over nothing.

7 August 1990

The following Tuesday, after I get home from work, my son is once again sitting in front of the television and watching the news. As I pass by the kitchen, I see Cindy sitting at the table with a cup of coffee.

"Hey, babe, what's up?" I ask cautiously.

"I guess you haven't heard the news?"

I walk into the living room and stand above my son, who looks up and, in a hyper way, says, "Hey, Dad. Marines landed in Saudi Arabia this morning. There's only a few hundred so far, but they're in Saudi Arabia, at the border, facing down the Iraqi Republican Guard. Cool."

I stare at Kevin then over my shoulder at Cindy, who stands at the kitchen entrance. She walks back in and sits down.

I raise my voice as I watch her walk away. "That doesn't mean anything, babe." I turn back and sit on the floor next to my son and watch TV.

8 August 1990

Today I learn Saddam Hussein annexed Kuwait, calling it part of Iraq, and the talk on the news is all about the world coming together against him. The buildup of American forces in Saudi

Arabia continues, but the president insists they are there only to ensure Saddam goes no farther. At the reserve center, the talk about the First Marine Division being on standby is only talk—so far.

15 August 1990

The buildup of US troops in Iraq continues as the rumors of war grow. The latest news report is from the Marine Corps, and they announce the commitment of forty-five thousand troops to the Persian Gulf area. This will include elements of the First Marine Expeditionary Force as well as units from the First Marine Division and the First Force Service Support Group, or FSSG. The First MEF is self-sustained, and those Marines deploy from ships. I remember from my time as company embarkation NCO that those forward ships are stocked with enough supplies to keep the troops in combat for thirty days.

But the First FSSG is the key for me. Having been in a support unit for the past ten years, I've learned that for the grunts, tanks, cannon cockers, or any combat unit to succeed, they need a strong support unit. That's where we come in. If the FSSG is going, it won't be long before they need us.

27 August 1990

It's Monday morning, and I'm driving my bread truck through the streets of Griffith, Indiana. I've already finished several of my smaller stops and am heading into Crown Point. Soon, I'll be at my wife's workplace.

If I time this right, I'll meet Cindy outside on her break. I hope she has a chocolate doughnut this time. She knows I love chocolate.

The sun shines brightly on this beautiful August morning. I pull in and park just as Cindy walks out the front door of her store. She's empty-handed, and there's no smile on her lips.

"What's wrong? It's a beautiful day. Are you having a problem at work?"

"Haven't you been listening to your radio?"

"No. My speaker's acting up. It's all static. I need to buy a new one. Why? What's going on?"

"The president has begun ordering up the reserves. The news says he'll order as many as two hundred thousand from all branches of service, beginning immediately." Tears fill her eyes. I take her into my arms, her head on my shoulder.

"I haven't heard anything. Let's not worry about anything until there's something to worry about, okay?"

She takes her head from my shoulder, looks into my eyes, and sniffles away her tears.

"I have to get back to work," she says. A quick kiss and Cindy returns to the store. I watch her walk away, then finish putting my order together.

With each passing day, it becomes more apparent our unit will soon be called to active duty. During the October drill, the platoon leaders and section heads meet to discuss the company's future. Major Bales explains, "It is my personal belief we'll all be on active duty soon. Today's Marine Corps functions on the premise that the reserves fill the holes the Corps has deliberately left vacant in order to have a larger combat-ready Marine Corps. Support units are where the reserves are needed." He scans our eyes, and we lock on his. "I have no actual orders to support any of this. But I firmly believe it will happen."

At home, I've tried to keep things normal, trying to not let on I know, sooner or later, my unit will be called into active duty. In bed one night, Cindy says, "Rick, we need to talk."

Those are words no man wants to hear, especially in bed. "What about?" I ask cautiously.

"About what happens if you get called up, into active duty."

"We don't know if that will ever happen and—"

"Shut up, will you!" Cindy barks.

I stop and stare, keeping my mouth shut.

In a softer voice, she says, "Just ... shut up. I want you to know something." Her eyes down, she says, "I've been going over this in my mind." Her eyes meet mine. "I married you, knowing you're a Marine. I'm proud of it. I know as a reservist, you can be called into active duty if we ever go to war." She laughs. "I never thought you would and still hope you won't."

Her eyes reveal something in her I've not seen before. Pride and something every Marine holds dear to his heart, *Semper Fidelis*. "But I think you will. I think this country is going to war, and you're going to fight." She pauses again to hold back the tears and looks straight into my eyes, saying, "When that time comes, I'll be the Marine Corps wife you need me to be. I'll send you off with hugs and kisses, but I won't hold you back with whimpering and begging you to stay. I will love you as you leave. I will honor you and the Marine Corps you serve as you go off to do your duty. And I'll do mine."

Now I'm the one trying to hold back tears as she continues.

"I just want you to know, I will do what you need me to do."

"I know, CJ. I always have."

"Do you remember when we were married, Rick? Do you remember our song?"

"Of course, Kenny Rogers and Dolly Parton, 'Island in the Stream.' It was our wedding song."

"Yes, it was. Those words meant the world to me back then, sweetheart, and they still do today." She leans in close to my face and sings some of the song into my ear.

I lean over and kiss her gently, pull back, and look into her eyes. I lean in again, and our lips touch. Our kiss is filled with passion, and the night turns into sensual pleasure.

3 November 1990

On the November drill weekend, both the first sergeant and I are called into Major Bale's office for a private meeting. He informs us he has taken the necessary actions to ensure the two of us will be going with him when the company is finally activated.

"You two are my combat veterans, and I need you with me. First Sergeant Wiśniewski and Staff Sergeant Green, your Vietnam experience will be put to the test when we finally deploy. We're going to be mobilized. I've been ordered to prepare the company for active duty. I'm informing certain personnel I believe have a … need to know. You two have that need to know. I don't have a date. It could be before the end of the year. It could be later. I don't know exactly, but we are going." The major pauses, giving us time to take in all he's said. "I do know half the company is going to the Persian Gulf, and the other half is going to the east coast."

"Why is that, sir?" I ask.

"I think it's because Headquarters Marine Corps expects heavy casualties, and they want a capable and ready reserve pool to fill the holes. They're being sent to Camp Lejeune, where they'll train to be ready. When we get to where we're sent, I'll do all I can to keep us together. However, I know that there'll be people in charge with other ideas and more rank than me. Get your affairs together, keep everything I just told you secret, and tell no one, not even your wives. Gentlemen, we're going to war."

The first sergeant and I walk out of the major's office.

"I'm surprised the major shared that information. I understand him sharing classified info with the XO and you, First Sergeant, but why me?"

The first sergeant doesn't answer. Clearly, his thoughts are elsewhere.

Away from any of the troops who might overhear us, I say, "Don, the last time you and I went to war, we were the ones depending on the higher rank to know what they were doing, to get us home alive. This time, these men are depending on us. Kind of scary, isn't it?"

"I know, Greeny. The troops will be depending on us. But we'll get them home."

"You know it, Top."

4 December 1990

It's a little past five in the morning, and I'm delivering to my first store when the manager stops me. "Your company just called and said you need to call your reserve center, immediately."

Using the manager's office phone, I call, and when they answer, I say, "This is Staff Sergeant Green. What's going on?"

"Staff Sergeant, Engineer Support Company has been

mobilized to active duty on four December 1990 at zero three hundred hours. You are to report immediately to your reserve unit. Do you acknowledge?"

I respond, "Affirmative."

CHAPTER 13

SAYING GOODBYE

I HANG UP THE PHONE AND try to figure what to do first. Call work? Yeah. They need to know what's happening.

Tommy, my driver supervisor, gets on the line, and immediately I realize he has no idea that was the military who contacted them, looking for me.

"What's going on, Rick? You mean that was the Marine Corps we talked to?"

"Remember, we talked about this, Tommy. I made you aware in the event my unit is called up during working hours. I said they'd contact you in order to have you reach me. That's what happened this morning."

"No, I didn't know. I wasn't here, and no one told me. What does all this mean?"

"It means I've been activated. I've been ordered to report for duty immediately, and I won't be able to finish the route. You'll have to get someone out here to pick up the truck. I'm at Friskies in Merrillville."

"You've been activated?"

"Yes, activated. I need to get moving. I have to get home, pack up my gear, and report for duty."

Finally understanding what's happening, Tommy doesn't argue. He understands what we both must do.

I hang up and prepare to call Cindy. She needs to know what's just happened, and I need to get to the reserve center. Telling her over the phone is not the way I envisioned this happening. Before

I can dial, the store manager, Jack, walks into his office. Out of courtesy, I try to explain what I'm doing.

"I've been called up for duty. All this crap going on with Iraq and Kuwait, the Marine Corps wants me."

"Jeez, that's terrible. I didn't even know you were in the Marines."

"Yep. Going on something like twenty years now, but what I really need to do is call my wife. I hate telling her over the phone, but what can I do? I need to get to my unit, like, right now. Can I continue to use your phone?"

"Of course, go right ahead." In a solemn tone, he says, "That can't be easy for her. Uh, where do you live, Rick?"

"No, it won't be easy. Crown Point. Why?"

"Would it be easier if I just give you a ride home?"

Without hesitation, I say, "Yes, it would. Thank you."

"It's the least I can do."

I'm in Jack's car and heading home to tell Cindy her fears have been realized. My stomach is in knots. I know she has dreaded the possibility of me going to war, and now it's happening. I don't know how to tell her. What can I say at a time like this that will make it any easier? And my kids. What about the kids? I feel the war may not go well. We lost fifty thousand in Vietnam, and this time it could be worse. Today might be the last time I see my family.

Arriving home before Cindy leaves for work, I step out of Jack's car and thank him, and he wishes me luck, saying, "My prayers will be with you, every day you're away."

"Thank you, Jack."

His car backs out of the driveway and heads down the street. I gaze upward, and a December sun is rising in a clear sky, its rays already thinning the morning dew. It's going to be a nice day.

I enter through the side door and go up the stairs. Cindy's in the kitchen, pouring a cup of coffee. Clearly surprised I'm home, she quickly looks out the window. "I don't see your truck. Where's your truck?"

"It's not here, CJ. I got a ride home from the Friskies store

79

manager." I'm trying to keep my emotions in check. I don't want to scare her, but I know this is something best just said.

She knows something's wrong. "What's going on?"

I'm silent for a few seconds more and then just tell her. "I've been activated."

Cindy stands still for a moment. There are no tears, no emotional outbursts. Controlling those sentiments, her face shows strength I didn't expect, but her eyes betray her. Cindy has trained herself for this moment and knows what she must do to be the Marine wife she needs to be. She's ready to send her Marine off to war and won't allow selfish emotions to interfere with his duty. Cindy knows what her burden is and will carry it.

"You have to report now?" she gently asks.

"Yes, immediately." After seeing the look in her eyes, my tone softens. "I'm a section leader. I need to be there to help coordinate the troops."

She looks at me calmly. "Let's get you packed," she says and walks toward the bedroom.

I follow her in. "I'll try to keep you up on what our schedule is. Let you know where we are and where we're going to be, as best I can. You'll have to get one of the kids to help you get the truck back from work. Don't let it sit there too long. It's not a good neighborhood."

"I'll have it back today." Then she asks, "What about the kids?"

"Better wake them so I can say goodbye."

The kids all see what is happening in the world and know my being called into active duty means I'm going to be involved in it. Kimberly, my oldest, is home from college and perhaps realizes it the most, but my son Kevin, who's sixteen and a sophomore in high school, says, "This is not an ATD."

Both Katie and Michael, each eleven, seem to know something is happening. Kimberly tries to reassure them. "Dad goes every year on those two-week things with the Marines, remember?" But Katie is taking it very hard, as she has always felt Dad would not come home. Dropping to her knees and holding Kate's arms while looking into her eyes, Kimberly adds, "He always comes back, doesn't he?"

Kevin bursts out, "This ain't any ATD, Kim. This is war Dad's going to."

Cindy gives Kevin a look that could kill, and he realizes he should have kept his mouth shut because now, Katie is shaking and scared. I take her in my arms and tell her, "Hey, everything's going to be all right. Don't be scared. I'll write you a lot, okay?"

She nods, and I wipe away her tears. Michael, my stepson, seems sad but is taking things as best as can be expected. Another hug from him and it's time to leave.

After all my goodbyes to the children, I finish packing my seabag and pull out my military-issued backpack the Marine Corps calls "Alice." It's short for "All-Purpose Lightweight Individual Carrying Equipment." Everything military goes in there. Once it's ready, I load it all into Cindy's car.

I know I should stop and say something to her. I know there are things that need to be said, but I don't say them. Cindy gets in the car, and I get behind the wheel.

I wave goodbye to the children one last time. They all stand at the side door except for Katie. She's alone at the kitchen window with tears in her eyes. Her tiny hand waves goodbye, and I give her a special smile. As I drive off, guilt comes over me because I know she's too young to understand what's happening.

Cindy and I speak no words until we're well under way, and even then, we don't talk about feelings. There's no time for that. We talk about important things like wills and insurance forms. I remind her, "While I'm away, the Soldiers and Sailors Act will protect you if the money gets tight. Remember, no one can shut anything off. Like the heat or electric. The mortgage company can't foreclose on you if you can't make the payments. And check into the lower-interest break they're supposed to give us as well."

"Stop, Rick! I know all that. I know about the electric company and the federal laws protecting us."

I listen, waiting for her next words, but they don't come. She's silent, and so am I. I don't know what to say or what she wants me to say. There's nothing left. More words now will only make the tears flow, and neither of us can afford that. She knows, as I do, we have to be strong.

"There's the center, CJ. We're here."

I pull in and stop the car in front of the headquarters building. Other Marines and their families are saying goodbye. The hustle and bustle tells us we have no time left. This is not something we can sit and watch. We have to keep moving.

I remove my seabag and Alice Pack from the car and watch as Cindy steps out. I walk around and stand in front of her, my hands on her arms. She looks deep into my eyes, and I know this could be the last time I hold her. Her tears no longer held back, she dissolves into my arms. Another squeeze is long and deep with passion. We kiss goodbye like lovers who will never see one another again. Looking in her tear-filled deep-blue eyes, I remember how I felt the day I first saw her, and now I'm the one holding back tears. One more kiss, just one more goodbye, and she gets in behind the steering wheel. Swinging my Alice Pack over my shoulders and on my back, I see the tears on her cheeks as she backs up the car. I fling the seabag over my shoulder. Walking toward headquarters, I hear the car engine, and I know she's leaving. Is she looking back?

Unable to continue without a final look goodbye, I turn, but she's gone. I look at the gate, but her car is nowhere in sight. Loneliness and sorrow overwhelm me. I didn't get one last look. I stare at the ground.

A Marine rushes past. "What's up, Staff Sergeant Green? We going to war?"

"Looks like it, Corporal Goodman. Sure looks like it."

CHAPTER 14

FIRST STOP, CAMP PENDLETON

I WALK THROUGH THE DOORS OF headquarters, putting Cindy and family out of my mind. The company is going to war, and I need to have my head in the game.

Captain Gable shouts out as he runs up the stairs, "Staff Sergeant Green, we're wanted in room two oh two. There's a company meeting for all staff and officers."

"Copy that, sir." Spotting one of my drivers walking down the stairs toward me, I say, "Lance Corporal Casey, take care of my gear."

"Copy that, Staff Sergeant."

I double-time past him up the stairs, taking two at a time. When I reach room 202, I walk in behind the captain. Inside I find an empty chair next to Staff Sergeant Woodlow. I've known Woody for more than two years, and he's my best friend. He's a little shorter than me, about five ten, and is a Marine of color. We share responsibility for Motor Transport Platoon. Woody's the section head for maintenance, as I am for the drivers. He's the best mechanic I've ever known in the Corps. We share an equal rank, but after Gunny Baylor became platoon commander, Motor T chief fell to me as a driver.

I look for but don't see my platoon commander. I lean over and whisper to Woody, "Hey, you seen Baylor?"

"Nope."

"He must be running late." It's more a statement than a question. Woody nods.

"I miss anything?"

"Just getting started."

"Gentlemen." Everyone quiets down as Major Bales begins. "First Sergeant Wiśniewski, are all staff and officers present?"

"Yes, sir, all present and accounted for."

The major is a well-built man about six two and, as always, has a pressed uniform. His high and tight haircut and spit-shined boots are something we've all come to expect, and today is no different.

"Staff Sergeant James, you are I and I Admin, correct?"

"Yes, sir."

"Are we ready to go? Paperwork completed? Record books up to date?"

"Yes, sir, the company is good to go."

"Who is in charge of our seven-eighty-two gear?"

The I & I supply chief responds, "I am, sir. All combat gear is stored in mount-out boxes and shipped along with the weapons."

"Good. Captain Gorman, do we have transportation arranged?"

Captain Gorman is the I & I commanding officer. His job is to ensure Major Bales has everything he needs to deploy.

"Yes, sir. Staff Sergeant Suduckey is in charge of transportation. Staff Sergeant, what do you have?"

"I've arranged for the buses to be here on six December at zero four hundred hours and be on the road by zero five hundred. Your plane flies out at eleven hundred. You'll have plenty of time, sir."

"What is our percentage of Marines on deck, Captain?"

"Before the meeting, we were at ninety-four percent. We have one hundred percent voice confirmation. All Marines activated will be on base by zero, zero, zero one tomorrow."

The major pauses a moment then asks, "Who will be in charge of weapons security?"

First Sergeant Wiśniewski interrupts, "Staff Sergeant Green, sir."

"Staff Sergeant Green?"

"Yes, sir."

"The armory will issue you a .45-caliber pistol. I'll give you a written order allowing you to carry the weapon in the airport and on the plane."

The major pauses for a moment then looks back at Gorman. "Do we have the written order, Captain?"

"Yes, sir, faxed in by battalion before the meeting. It's awaiting your signature."

"Good. Staff Sergeant, the weapons will not leave your sight until secured in the belly of the plane. Is that understood?"

"Aye, aye, sir."

"If you're not yet aware, Gunny Baylor is not part of Sixth Engineers Battalion Forward. You're the acting platoon commander for Motor Transport. At least until we reach Saudi Arabia."

I raise my eyebrows with the news Gunny Baylor won't be coming with us and respond, "Copy that, sir."

The major stands and addresses us. "Men, we are going to war. Some of those Marines downstairs will not be coming back, hopefully most will." As he pauses, I watch his eyes move across each of us. "Some in this room may not come back. You know what's expected of you. Remember who we are. You are well trained. Do your jobs. Until we leave, I want a tight ship. We'll be staying two nights in a local hotel. There will be no drinking by anyone, which includes staff and officers. Our chow is being catered to the reserve center. Transportation to the hotel will be by motor transport. Staff Sergeant Green, make that happen."

I respond, "Aye, aye, sir."

"Does anyone have a question?" The room is silent. "No? Dismissed."

The staff and officers file out. I head downstairs to get my platoon in order and arrange for the hotel transportation.

The next two days, Motor T gets all the company vehicles ready for shipment to Southwest Asia. We are now part of the largest sea bridge invasion since World War II.

6 December 1990

Our buses arrive at O'Hare, and an airline employee escorts me to the tarmac. The plane's engines are running, and the smell of burning fuel flashes me back to Vietnam. I watch the weapons transferred to the Delta DC-9 and walk up the steps through the tail end of the plane. All the Marines on board are quiet. Everyone's tired. A few civilians are on board with us. They seem anxious, maybe wondering why we're here. The .45 on my hip draws a lot of attention. I smile, and they smile back. Near the front of the plane, I find Staff Sergeant Woodlow and sit. Moments later, the aircraft begins to taxi and is soon airborne.

After landing in LA, I escort our weapons to the Marine Corps Base Camp Pendleton armory. There, I hand over my .45 and receive a release of responsibility for the rifles.

We're billeted in some old wooden two-story barracks. The major wastes no time before he starts training. He takes the company on a ten-mile night hump.

On day two, Motor Transport Platoon begins to off-load civilian trucks from across the nation. They're hauling everything from road graders to bulldozers, from water purification units to electric generators, all destined for Saudi Arabia.

22 December 1990

I'm talking on the phone. "No, Cindy, I still don't know when we're supposed to go."

"Will you still be there for Christmas?"

"Yes. I've been told we'll get a forty-eight-hour pass for both Christmas Eve and Christmas Day. But our pass is only good for a one-hundred-mile radius. I can't come home."

"I'm flying out. Don't try to stop me. Call me back in an hour, and I'll give you the details. Goodbye."

The phone goes dead. I have no intention of stopping her. In fact, I'm happy she's coming. An hour later, I call her back.

"Sweetheart," Cindy says, "I arrive on the twenty-fourth at nine o'clock in the morning, and guess what?"

"What?"

"You know my cousin, Brandon? Who lives in LA?"

"No, I don't. Who?"

"Brandon. Never mind. My mother called him, and he wants to help." Laughing, she says, "He arranged for a suite at the Beverly Hilton Hotel in downtown Los Angeles. We've got both Christmas Eve and Christmas night booked and paid for."

"Why's your cousin doing this?"

"He's rich and wants to show support for the troops. Everything is taken care of. We'll have room service, everything."

On the twenty-fourth, I meet Cindy at the airport. The next two days are heavenly bliss. On Christmas Eve, we take a ride to Rodeo Drive and visit such famed stores as Louis Vuitton and Tiffany. That night, we dine at the hotel restaurant, Circa 55, and end the evening with a carriage ride around the city, taking in all the holiday decorations. On Christmas Day, we stay in our hotel room, most of the time in bed. With room service on her cousin's dime, we indulge in fine wine and more exceptional dining.

In bed, I decide to share my dream. "I have something to tell you, something that's bothered me since I was activated."

She stares, puzzled, as I continue.

"Do you remember when I went to Hawaii?"

She looks suspicious, as if I'm about to drop a bombshell like infidelity.

"No! No, not that."

"Then what?" she asks.

"When I flew out there, I fell asleep on the plane. It was a long flight." I tilt my head from side to side, wondering whether I should continue. "I had a dream I was in a desert war." Looking into her eyes, I come right out and say, "In the dream … I died."

Cindy begins to look worried. "After I died, I go to heaven, or hell, I'm not sure, and I—"

"Stop! Please stop." With a tear running down her cheek, she asks, "Why did you have to tell me this now? Our last night together, and you ruin it with you're going to die?" She gets out of bed and walks to the bar, where she pours herself a double shot of tequila. She turns back and stares then shoots the alcohol in one sweeping move, straight down her throat.

"Do you know how many times I've dreamt you're never coming back? Do you know why I'm here?" She walks to the bed and sits down. In a soft voice, she says, "Because I felt this could be the last time we're together."

While she sobs, I say, "I'm sorry, CJ. I want you to understand what could happen."

She chokes back the tears. "I know you may not come home. I'm not stupid or naive. I know people die in war." Her eyes filled with love, she says, "Hold me. Love me like this will be the last time."

Wiping her tears away, I take her in my arms. The softness of her face, the warmth of her body, the gentleness of her lips is all around me. We fall back on the bed, and our love fills us with passion until we finally fall asleep in each other's arms.

Later that night, I wake from another nightmare. I get up and go to the head, splashing cool water on my face. Walking out, I see Cindy lying asleep. I move to her side of the bed and gently sit, not wanting to wake her. Her hair lies across her face, and I softly move it aside. I touch her arm. It's warm and soft. She stirs but doesn't wake. I watch as every breath she takes makes me realize how much I love her and how I will miss her.

This is the last time I'll be with you, CJ. The last time I'll see you sleeping. I love you, baby.

I stand and walk to the balcony, looking out at a city filled with lights. A cold chill covers me, and I whisper, "This is my fate. This is how I'm supposed to die."

Oh, Bubba, I'll be seeing you soon, my friend ... real soon.

7 January 1991

By 0100 we're leaving LA and flying to New York. There we transfer to a 747 airliner, which begins our final leg to Saudi Arabia. Being an E-6 has its privileges. Staff Sergeant Woodlow and I get to sit in the business section in large recliner seats, two to an aisle. They're so comfortable, not like the small economy seats the troops have in the back of the plane. In these seats, we can lie flat with a full extension of our legs. So nice.

It's a long flight across the ocean. Our first stop is Italy, where we refuel. We're told to stay in our seats. Outside, Italian soldiers surround the aircraft, and when the flight attendant opens the hatch, an armed Italian steps inside. I lean over to Woody and say, "This is like a movie."

The refueling is complete, and the plane is airborne again. More boring hours go by, and I begin to wonder how my men are doing. I get up and walk to check on them, something I've done more than once during this flight.

"It won't be long now," I say. "A couple more hours and we'll be there. If you guys want something, just ask the flight attendants. They'll get you anything they have."

I return to my seat. An hour later, the pilot announces over the intercom, "We'll be landing at Al Jabar airfield soon. For myself and on behalf of the flight crew, we want to wish you all good luck and let you know your country stands with you. Semper Fi, Marines."

The sounds of "Ooh Rah!" ring out.

CHAPTER 15

ARRIVAL

7 January 1991
0900 hours

AL JUBAIL. THE NAME IS as foreign as the sights outside my window. Our 747 circles, and below I see an airfield with a single airstrip. Three walled barricades protect fighter jets parked along the side of the runway. I can't tell if they're ours or those of the Saudi Air Force.

This airfield is military.

Beyond the buildings and the hardened landing strip is a vastness I've never seen from the sky. I've seen sand before but have never experienced such a massive expanse of nothing, and that's what it is—nothing but sand.

As the plane continues to descend, the winds move the land as if it's alive. Its color is eerie, a reddish yellow, not like in California. It's somehow different here.

The plane touches down then slows to a stop. Two Hummers carrying Marines drive up to the plane. The first sergeant, who's been sitting across from Woody and me, stands. "Gather your shit together. Once off the plane, get your platoons into formation."

While grabbing my gear from the overhead bin, I ask, "You ready? This is it, Woody."

"You know it, man."

The hatch nearest Woody and me opens, and we step out. The sun is bright, but the air is cool, not a dry heat like I expected.

Down the stairs and on the ground, I spot Major Bales standing next to one of the camouflaged Hummers.

"Check out the inverted V on the Hummer door, Woody."

"What's that about?"

"That identifies the vehicle as being American, or Allied."

From the tail end of the plane, I watch my Marines exit. As they do, they begin to mill around in a clusterfuck.

I need to get them organized.

"Let's go, Woody. We need to find Ford."

Sergeant Ford is a lanky thirty-year-old Marine of color who grew up on the near south side of Chicago. He's a good Marine and my platoon sergeant.

"Get these people in formation, Sergeant. We need to be ready to move out, ASAP." Turning to Woody, I ask, "Hey, man, did you know Bales would be here waiting for us?"

"Shit no. I thought he was on the plane."

"Hell, man. I thought the same thing. You know, I don't remember seeing him after we got back from the forty-eight-hour Christmas liberty."

Woody nods.

We're off the plane, and the major talks with the officers who flew in. "Staff Sergeant Green, follow Warrant Officer Coleman to the staging area."

"Copy that. When we getting our weapons, First Sergeant?"

"As soon as we're in company formation. They'll be issued by platoon."

"Do we have ammo?"

"Not yet. The buses are on the way, so we'll be outta here ASAP."

Warrant Officer Coleman marches his platoon off the tarmac, and I have Motor T trail right behind him. We march a hundred yards from the plane and stop another twenty-five yards off the runway. Moments later, two Hummers arrive carrying all the company gear.

First Sergeant Wiśniewski holds a quick meeting with the platoon commanders. "We'll issue seven-eighty-two gear first. The most important thing your Marines need to have is their gas masks. Anything else missing, we'll reissue from the unit we're assigned to. Gas masks are in short supply."

"We getting ammo for the weapons, First Sergeant?"

With a stern look in my direction, he says, "No! There isn't any, Staff Sergeant. We'll have to wait until we get to Mishab. That's where we're going."

"Isn't where we're going a hostile area? You know, bad guys? We need ammo for our rifles."

"There is no ammo for us here. Quit your bitching and get your troop's gear inventoried!"

I quiet down and stare at the first sergeant. After he walks away, I yell, "Sergeant Ford."

"Yeah, Staff."

"Get the seven-eighty-two gear distributed. Make sure each man has his gas mask. If anyone does not, I need to know ASAP."

"Copy that." He walks away.

It's 1130 when two Marines, sent by Command, walk up to me carrying Meals Ready to Eat, or MREs. One asks, "This Motor Transport?"

I answer, "Yeah. Those for us?"

"Believe it, Staff Sergeant."

"Corporal Goodman, take charge of this chow. When the buses get here, put them on board. Do not issue any meals until we're under way."

"Copy that."

With the chow and the 782 gear complete, Sergeant Ford assures me all our Marines have their gas masks. Next I distribute the platoon weapons, and Motor T is good to go.

Transportation arrives, and I notice the bus drivers are all Arabic. I'm a little bothered by this but shake it off.

Ain't nothing but a thing.

The First Sergeant is alone when I walk over. "Don, what's our destination again?"

"Mishab. Eighth Engines has been there since October."

"Is that a town or something?"

"Yeah, it is, but that's not where we're going. Not the town. Someplace in the desert."

"Mishab ... hmm. How far from here?"

"Eighty miles, maybe more. It's east. It'll take a few hours to get there. Most of the drive is through the desert."

"Interesting. I hate to keep asking, man, but we need ammo."

"I told you, there isn't any for us."

"So we're traveling down dangerous roads in buses driven by Arabs, who might hate us, and we won't even know if we're going in the right direction. And we have no ammunition?"

"That's right. You have your .45."

"A single handgun. Not much help, Don."

"The major knows the way to Mishab. We'll be okay. He was there yesterday. Are your people ready?"

"They are."

"Then start getting them aboard. I'll tell the major the company is ready to move out."

The platoon on the bus, Staff Sergeant Woodlow and I sit in the front seat, across the aisle from Major Bales.

"Your men doing okay, Staff Sergeant Green?" the major asks.

"Yes, sir, good to go."

"What about you, Staff Sergeant? What's your name again?"

"Woodlow, sir, maintenance chief."

"You're part of Motor Transport Platoon?"

"Yes, sir. Staff Sergeant Green and I work together."

The major nods and shifts his attention to some papers lying next to him.

"Corporal Goodman, you have the MREs?" I shout.

"Yes, Staff Sergeant."

As the buses roll down the road, I walk to his seat then turn and ask Woody, "Staff Sergeant Woodlow, what MRE do you want?"

"Chicken and dumplings."

"Major, how about you?"

"I'm good."

"Copy that," I reply in a hushed voice. "Give me spaghetti

and hand out the MREs." I take the two MREs to my seat, where Woody and I chow down.

An hour into our trip, we pull off the hard surface road, and the other bus takes the lead. A cloud of dust from his rear tires causes our driver to fall back.

Out the window, the Arabian civilized world disappears until all that is left is an empty desert. There are no plants, no animals, nothing but sand. Ahead of us is a trail of powder billowing upward from the other bus.

Without warning, the bus comes to a stop. Pointing at his watch, the driver tries to communicate with the major. He reaches behind his seat and pulls out a small rolled rug. After leaving the bus, he sets it on the ground, kneels on it, and begins to pray. From the back of the bus, some young Marine yells out, "Give the towel head an MRE."

Another one adds, "Yeah, and make it pork." The Marines all laugh, and I understand they're young and unsure of what is ahead of them. Making crude jokes helps them hide their fear. Back in my time, I'm sure I was no different. It's how we faced the unknown.

I turn to the seat behind me. "Sergeant Ford, when the driver gets back in the bus, give him an MRE. Not pork. You got it?"

"Copy that, Staff."

The driver finishes praying, rolls up his prayer rug, and returns to his seat. Sergeant Ford offers him an MRE. He accepts it, smiling, and we're under way again.

It's 1900 when I look out the windshield and notice the lead bus is no longer in sight. We're alone on the desert road. In the growing darkness, the driver turns on the bus's headlights, and a hundred feet of road ahead lights up.

Behind me, the Marines all fall quiet. The rowdy behavior has stopped, and most are asleep. I see Woody is asleep as well, but not the major. In the darkness, I lean toward him and ask, "Sir, what does Mishab look like?"

In a low voice, he answers, "It's big. You have Eighth Engines and Seventh Motor T Battalion. Second Medical Battalion and elements of Seventh Engineers is there as well. Surrounding the whole place is a ten-foot-high berm made of sand."

"Who we getting attached to? I heard Eighth."

"You heard right. Sixth Engineers will no longer exist for us."

Woody wakes and asks, "How come not the Seventh, sir? That's who we worked with in Pendleton."

"General Krulak wants the Eighth reinforced. They've been here since November and tasked with building both Mishab and Tikrit. They've been working shorthanded, and he wants them up to full strength." He pauses. "The Eighth is going to play a major role in the invasion."

With no warning, the bus bounces hard, throwing a few Marines out of their seats. The vehicle swerves to the right and comes to a stop off the road. Standing, I yell, "Is everyone all right?"

"Yeah, Staff Sergeant, good to go," one of them answers.

"What the hell happened?" I ask.

"We must have hit a bump," the major says.

The driver attempts to get us moving again, but it's useless. We're stuck.

The driver is off the bus to assess the damage, and the major is right behind him. Woodlow and I follow them off.

I tell Sergeant Ford to stay on the bus and maintain order. Outside, we check the drive tires. They're buried in the sand.

"We're not going anywhere without a wrecker, sir," Woody says.

Inside the bus, the Marines have gotten loud, and they're arguing.

I stick my head inside, yelling, "What the hell, Sergeant? What's going on?"

"You ain't gonna believe this, but we have ammo."

"What!" I climb back in. "Explain."

"Lance Corporal Edman has five boxes, a hundred rounds."

"Who is Edman?"

"He's Heavy Equipment, at the back of the bus. He won't give it up."

Walking to the rear, I find the Marine. "You got ammo?"

He nods.

"Where did you get these rounds?" He says nothing, but his

look of defiance says enough. "You could be charged with having contraband or stealing government property."

"I didn't steal anything," he fires back.

Loud and firm, I ask again, "Then where?"

Letting out a breath of air, he grudgingly answers. "While we were back at the airport. A guy I know from boot camp is with the air wing. He said he had some extra rounds and gave these to me." He shows me the ammo.

"Give them up now, Lance Corporal!"

He hands them over, adding, "This is bullshit."

Giving my attention to Ford, I hand him the five boxes while lowering my voice. "He's right. This is bullshit. No one could find ammo for us, but this Marine got a hundred rounds and didn't even have to sign for them."

"What do you want me to do?"

"Take ten magazines and load them with ten rounds each. Distribute them to motor transport Marines. We're going to be here awhile, and I'm not sure if everyone using this road is friendly. Take four men and post one on each corner of the outer perimeter. Take the other six and form a three sixty around the bus. Make sure you're one of those with loaded mags. Concertina wire is a few yards off the road on our right. Keep everyone away from there. No one goes beyond the road. I saw armed guards walking around on the other side. I don't want anyone getting dead from friendly fire."

"Aye, aye, Staff Sergeant."

"Wait one, Ford." I stop to think for a minute. "Get four Marines. Put an empty magazine in each of their weapons then bolt home. Post one with each of the four men on the corners. I don't want men that far from the main body alone. It'll look like we're all packing ammo."

"Aye, aye, Staff."

Staff Sergeant Woodlow yells from outside, "Staff Sergeant Green."

"What is it, man?"

"It's the major. He's going over the wire."

"What!" I barrel out of the bus, Woody fast on my tail.

"I tried to stop him. He won't listen."

In a panic to reach the major in time, I blurt out, "He's gonna get killed."

CHAPTER 16

DANGER IN THE DESERT

Still 7 January 1991

MOVING AS FAST AS I can to reach the CO before he crosses into danger, I stumble to the ground. After picking myself up, I'm off again. Spotting him as he begins to step over the wire, I yell out, "Sir, stop!"

Turning abruptly, he answers, "What's wrong, Staff Sergeant?"

"Don't go in there, sir."

"We need help, and I can see people walking."

"Yes, sir, those are walking guard posts, and they're carrying weapons. I doubt they speak English, and if they challenge you, sir, do you know the password?"

To my relief, the major heads back. "Maybe you're right, but we still need help. Do you think we can dig ourselves out?"

"Maybe, sir, but those wheels have sunk in deep."

"Get some men and try. We can't stay here. I'm not sure what might come down that road."

"Copy that, Major. Sergeant Ford!" I shout.

"Yes, Staff Sergeant."

"Get a squad down here and start digging out those tires. And don't forget about the front ones too."

"Copy that."

While a dozen Marines attempt to dig the bus out, I explain to the major how I came up with the ammunition.

"Lance Corporal Edman, he's from Heavy Equipment. He

managed to find a hundred rounds, sir. I confiscated them and passed out ten rounds each to ten Marines."

After mulling over the story, the major says, "When we get to Mishab, make sure your people keep that ammo. Don't let anyone know you have it. I'm not sure what we're going to be issued. Right now, everything is going to the grunts. Supplies are behind schedule. There may not be enough ammunition for troops considered nonessential."

This news bothers me. I'm not used to being in a combat zone where there isn't enough ammo for everyone. In Vietnam, we had so much ammunition we could waste it on a Fourth of July celebration.

Now, there isn't enough to go around?

Without looking beyond the immediate area, the major asks, "How's our security, Green?"

"I set up a three sixty around the bus and covered the corners of our outer perimeter with two-man sentries. Anything not friendly tries to get in, we'll handle it."

He looks around and agrees. "Defense looks good. You have it under control. That's why I wanted you with me, Staff Sergeant."

"Copy that, sir."

It's 2100, and nothing has come down the road. Using only their hands, the men are removing as much sand from the tires as possible. The major determines we've done all we can. The driver gets in the bus and tries to move it back to the road. After moving only a few inches, the tires start to spin. The sand is too soft.

Without a wrecker, we're not going anywhere.

"Secure the men, Staff Sergeant. We'll figure something else out."

"Aye, aye, sir."

Staff Sergeant Woodlow comes out of the bus and reminds me, "These Marines are not combat tested. They're carrying loaded weapons. We don't want an accidental discharge."

"You're right, Woody. You take the corners. I'll take the

men around the bus. Make sure they understand unless there are weapons firing, they stay calm and wait for orders. The last thing we want is someone to open fire."

At 2130, one of the guards alerts me to a pair of headlights approaching. "Staff Sergeant, we got company. What do we do?" a nervous Marine asks.

"Stand ready!" I yell back.

I pull my .45 from its holster and hold it at my side. My thumb pulls back the hammer. Two Marines with rifles are close by. One guard is next to the CO and me, the other a few feet away. This will put the oncoming vehicle between us.

The major seems to be thinking out loud when he says, "The other bus has to be at Mishab by now. Maybe this is one of ours coming to look for us."

Ours or not, we're stopping whoever it is.

The bus headlights cast a pale glow on the oncoming vehicle. Enough so I can tell it's military by the whip antenna bent over from the back and tied down to the front bumper.

I yell out, "It's military, sir. And they have a radio!"

As I hold my hand up, the driver slows, and I see the inverted *V* on the vehicle's hood. "They're one of us, sir," I call out with a sense of relief. "They have the *V*." The vehicle comes to a stop between my guard, the major, and me.

The man inside the car asks, "Are you having a problem, mate?"

The major, hearing him speak and recognizing he's British, moves closer to the vehicle. "Yes, Captain, we are. Our bus is stuck. We need to let our people at Mishab know where we are and send a wrecker to pull us out. Can you help?"

"Mishab is only twenty kilometers down the road." Looking over his shoulder, he says, "Corporal, get HQ on the line and have them contact the Americans in Mishab. Which unit, Major?"

"Eighth Engineers."

"Did you get that, Corporal?"

He nods.

"Tell HQ a detachment of US Marines are stuck along the

side of the road, twenty kilometers west of Mishab. They need a wrecker. That should do it."

"Thank you, Captain."

"Wish you luck, Major. We need to be on our way. A bit of a warning for you, though. There have been reports of terrorists on this road. Be on the lookout, won't you? Cheerio, then." And they were gone.

Curious, I ask, "How did you know his rank, sir?"

"Three gold triangles with an inner red circle. All in line is a captain in the British Army."

"I'll have to remember that, sir."

I turn and watch the British vehicle drive into the desert night. The vastness surrounding us is quiet, broken only by the hum of our bus's motor. We leave it running to keep the headlights on. That same hour, another vehicle approaches. As it comes into range and begins to pass the Marines guarding the northeast corner, it slows to a crawl.

"Looks like civilians inside, Staff Sergeant," a guard says. The closer the vehicle gets to my raised hand, the more the occupants become visible. Without taking my eyes off them, I inform the CO, "Major! They're all armed."

CHAPTER 17

MISHAB

"JUSTIN! MOORE!"

"Yes, Staff Sergeant."

"Split your ranks. Moore to the outside, Justin with the major and me. Weapons at the ready."

The two Marines move as ordered. Once again, I'll keep the oncoming vehicle between two armed Marines.

I can see the major's concern. It's the same as mine. I ask, "How do you want to handle this, sir?"

"Let them come between us but stop them."

"Copy that." I move to the center and raise my hand.

As the vehicle nears, the occupants become visible. Their weapons are butt down on the floor and not threatening. The driver slows then stops inches from me.

The major approaches the vehicle's driver's side. "Who are you?"

The man behind the wheel answers in Arabic.

I glance over at PFC Maurice. "Keep your eye on those men in the back seat, Maurice."

"Copy that, Staff Sergeant."

The driver's attention is on the major. The others in the vehicle stare at the Marines pointing their M-16s at them. One of the men in the back seat starts yelling at the major. The driver tries to calm him. When he raises his weapon in a hostile manner, I bring up my .45, pointing it at him. "Don't do anything stupid!" I yell.

The Marines around me react, bringing their rifles to deadly force.

"Hold your fire!" the major yells. "We're US Marines. Lower your weapons. Everyone!"

My men wait for me to bring down the .45, and then they follow, lowering their weapons back to alert. The driver of the vehicle screams at the man in the back seat. When the irritated one sees we're at ease, he lowers his voice, and his weapon.

The driver, now speaking English, says to the major, "He doesn't like you here, in our country. He's okay now."

"So you do speak English. Why did you answer me in Arabic?"

"Not sure who you were. These are dangerous times, yes?"

"Yes, these are dangerous times," the major answers. "Tell your man we don't like being in your country either."

The major orders, "Let them go, Staff Sergeant."

I stare at the major then reply, "Aye, aye, sir." As they pull away, I ask, "Sir, how do you know they're not terrorists? Those Brits said—"

"Yesterday, command officers had a meeting with General Krulak. He explained the civilians in the Mishab area are Saudi and will most likely be carrying weapons. He advised us to treat them as friendly. He added to not take any aggressive action toward them but always stay alert when they're around." He pauses a moment, looking down the road then at me. "I have no idea if they are or are not terrorists. But we do not need a confrontation tonight." While his eyes are still following the departing vehicle, he adds, "Stay alert … in case they double back."

I turn and watch the taillights fade away, and then, from Mishab, another vehicle approaches. It's still a ways off, but the height of the headlights tells me it's a truck.

"This looks like our wrecker coming, sir."

An M939 wrecker stops where I'm standing. A corporal sticks his head out the window, asking, "You need a tow, Staff Sergeant?"

The major answers, "Corporal, I need you to pull this bus out."

"Aye, aye, sir."

"Staff Sergeant Woodlow, get everyone out of the bus."

"Copy that, sir."

I watch as the driver backs his vehicle up to the front of the bus, gets out, and attaches chains to the axle. He connects the boom hook to the chains and pulls it tight. Once in his cab, he moves his vehicle forward, pulling the bus back on the road. Within minutes, the wrecker has done its job. After unhooking the boom, we're ready to go. Taking his time to talk with the truck driver, the CO is the last to board the bus.

The major informs us, "The wrecker will lead us the rest of the way in."

After our twenty-minute drive, the base comes into view. The first thing I notice is a ten-foot-high sand berm with a guard post raised at the corner. The berm runs along the road, and behind that barrier is our new unit.

The wrecker driver stops at the entrance to talk with the guards. Waved through, the bus follows, and we enter Mishab. We come to a stop in front of a large tent marked "Eighth Engineers, Battalion Headquarters."

Seeing the major greeted by a captain, I'm off the bus and walking up to the two officers. Interrupting them, I ask, "By your leave, sir, where do we go?"

The major turns. "Captain Morrison, this is Staff Sergeant Green. He's the acting platoon commander and our Motor T chief."

The captain extends his hand, and we shake. The major continues, "Captain Morrison will be your platoon commander."

"Outstanding, sir," I reply.

The captain calls a Marine over. "Sergeant Brown, take these men to where they're billeted." To me, he says, "We'll talk in the morning, Staff Sergeant."

"Copy that, sir."

The major and the captain walk into the headquarters.

"Sergeant Ford, get everyone off the bus and in formation," I command.

"As soon as you're ready, Staff Sergeant, you can follow me."

When everyone is off the bus, we follow the sergeant. As we do, I try to familiarize myself with the base, but the absence of light makes it impossible.

"Are we in blackout condition, Sergeant?" I ask.

"Yes, and have been for our entire time here."

"How long is that?"

"Thirty days. Come on. This way."

As we near the area for billeting, I notice all the general-purpose tents are in dugouts. These dugouts look deep enough to cover almost the entire tent.

Protection against an artillery strike. Interesting.

Stopping at one of the tents, the sergeant says, "This one is for you and your men."

Sergeant Brown leads us down a footpath dug out between the sand walls surrounding the tent. With a red bulb flashlight in hand, he steps inside, warning us, "Everyone in. Close up the hatchway. Remember, we're in a blackout."

Once everyone is inside, he flips a switch, and light from an electric light bulb fills the tent. His job done, he flips the light off and leaves.

"Someone flip the lights back on." The tent illuminated, I explain our situation. "We rough it tonight, people. There's enough racks for everyone, so claim one and get some sleep. We'll see about bedding tomorrow. Sergeant Ford, get me a head count and then lights out."

"Copy that, Staff."

Coolness, unexpected in the desert, finds its way into the tent, chilling my bones. After Ford completes his roster, I find a rack at the front and lie down fully dressed. I use my field jacket as a blanket and my gas mask as a pillow.

8 January 1991

I lie awake on my cot, waiting for the day to begin. Sergeant Brown walks in, allowing the brightness of the day to flood the tent. "We have a formation outside, Staff Sergeant. Have your men fall in."

I nod and see Sergeant Ford is waking the Marines. Slipping my field jacket on and leaving my 782 gear, I step outside. A formation of about twenty-five men and women Marines are already assembled. A master sergeant stands at their front.

Noticing me, he calls out, "Have your people fall in, Staff Sergeant."

"Aye, aye, Master Sergeant."

My eighteen Marines, nine mechanics, and nine drivers fall in as two squads at the rear. Off to the side is Captain Morrison. He walks to the front and addresses the platoon.

"I want to welcome those Marines who joined us last night. You men are part of this platoon. You are no longer reservist, you are active duty. We're all Marines here. Our job starts now. Make sure all our trucks are roadworthy. Tomorrow we'll begin moving equipment from the Al Jabar port back to here. There's a lot to do, so be ready for some heavy miles."

The platoon answers, "Ooh Rah!"

"Sergeant Brown?"

"Yes, sir."

"Take Staff Sergeant Green's people to supply for MREs and ammunition. Platoon ... dismissed."

As I begin to leave with my men, the captain asks, "Staff Sergeant, stick around for a few minutes. I want to go over what our mission is. Have you met Master Sergeant Howard?"

"No, sir, not yet."

The captain calls the master sergeant over and introduces us, then he explains our mission and how it will work. "Master Sergeant Howard is our Motor T chief. You, Staff Sergeant, will be in control of convoy operations. Major Bales has high praise for you. That's why I'm putting you in charge. Also, the fact you're a Vietnam combat veteran makes my decision easier." He continues, "Keep this confidential. I don't want the troops to know what I'm about to explain. When the ground war starts, we're going to have casualties. Command warns us to expect losses in the thousands. This war is not going to be a cakewalk. Mishab can be in range of Iraqi mobile artillery in minutes, and we're still vulnerable to air attack. Major Shepard is the company CO. He wants a staff NCO to bunk with the troops, so that's where you'll be. He feels if we're attacked, a staff NCO will have better control of the men."

My expression seems to have the captain puzzled.

"You disagree, Staff Sergeant?"

"Yes, sir. I don't think a staff NCO will make any difference. The sergeants and corporals are who we need to show our confidence in. They can do the job, sir."

"You may be right, but the major's in command. We do it his way."

"Aye, aye, sir."

When the captain walks away, the master sergeant and I move toward a tent used as the Motor T office. Howard asks, "Who were you with in 'Nam, Staff Sergeant?"

"First Recon Battalion, '69 to '70. How about you? Were you in 'Nam?"

"Yes, I was. Truck Company, Headquarters Battalion, First Marine Division, 1967 to '68."

I throw in an Ooh Rah then add, "The captain said my men will be receiving ammunition. I heard there was a possibility none is available."

"Yesterday, that was true. Ammo arrived late last night, somewhere around zero dark thirty. Now, each man receives a hundred sixty rounds."

"Not even a firefight."

"Better than nothing," the master sergeant says.

Without warning, a loud siren screeches, causing me to tighten my muscles and turn my head. Looking all around, I yell, "What the hell is that?"

Removing his cover and gripping it tightly, he shouts back, "It's a gas attack. Everyone get into their MOPP suits."

In shock, I say, "What the hell! We don't have any."

I see my men are confused, and not knowing what to do, I yell, "Get your gas masks on!"

CHAPTER 18
MISHAB TO JABAR

THE WARNING ECHOES ACROSS MISHAB. The siren changes to short blasts and continues for a few more minutes. The possibility of a chemical gas attack on my first day sends images of what-could-be flashing through my mind, but I need to keep my head. I see panic in my Marines. They need to get to their gas masks. I run to the tent we slept in last night to find my mask while yelling, "Get in the tent! Get to your masks!"

My men follow me in, and I order, "Don your masks. Hurry. Be sure to clear them and get a good seal." Taking my mask from its carry case while I'm under pressure, I fumble with the straps but get it on. I clear it by placing my hand over the front mouthpiece and blowing out. Next, I place both hands over the filters and breathe in. The tightness of the mask assures me it's sealed. I'm now breathing purified air.

I look across the tent and see the Marines frantically placing their masks over their faces and clearing them, just as they've been trained to do. All except PFC Tilly. A young Marine just eighteen years old, his eyes bulging and not blinking, he's frozen in fear. I move quickly to his side. "Get ahold of yourself." I grab the mask from his fumbling fingers, straighten out the straps, then order, "Put it on." He follows my directions. I yell, "Clear your mask, Marine!" He clears the mask and begins to calm as he looks me in the eye. Turning away, I tell the men, "That siren means we're under a gas attack. Everyone stays in the tent until I figure out what the hell is going on." It worries me to step outside without a MOPP suit on, but I do because I need to know.

Going outside, I see Marines with gas masks on and carrying their chemically protected MOPP suits. *How the hell did we get into a MOPP 1 status? What the hell happened to MOPP 0? I need to find a staff NCO or an officer. What are we supposed to do?* I'm searching for any info I can when I hear the call, "All clear, all clear." Removing my mask, I exhale with a real sense of relief. Sticking my head back in the tent, I inform the troops, "It's over. You can take your masks off and come outside."

As the men trail out, each has his mask in its casing and attached to his utility belt. The Marines are mumbling about not having MOPP suits. I don't blame them. With the danger of gas, they should have had them last night. What if we had gone to MOPP 2 or worse? What if this had been an actual gas attack?

Sergeant Brown walks by carrying a MOPP suit and wearing his gas mask. My eyes cold and hard, I yell, "Sergeant! We need to get to Supply. Just point me in the right direction. I'll take care of this myself."

"No problem, Staff." After removing his mask, he hands me the paperwork needed to receive our gear and points at Supply.

Standing next to me, Woody asks, "What the hell was that all about?"

"Gas attack, I guess. Come on, man. We're getting our shit."

Together we take the platoon to a half-buried twenty-foot-long shipping container. A sergeant sits in the doorway on a gray folding chair and uses ammo crates for a desk. Behind him, two PFCs sit on the deck, his helpers. Still pissed off, I walk up and hand him the requisition forms. "We arrived last night. I need MOPP suits and whatever else you have for these Marines."

He takes the forms and asks, "How many Marines do you have?"

"Eighteen enlisted and two staff NCOs."

"Have each man fill in his name at the top of these sheets and sign the bottom. I'll do the rest."

I take the forms and pass them out, explaining what to do. I ask the sergeant, "You have any pens?" He gives me a handful, and I pass them on to the men.

Once we're done, the sergeant quickly looks through the paperwork and begins distributing the gear. The first thing we're given is ten boxes of MREs. He explains, "This is your chow for the next six days. One box for two Marines."

"We're down to two meals a day?" I ask.

"There's hot food on the other side of the base. They serve one meal a day, at noon. The line gets long, and it takes twenty minutes to walk, so start early."

We receive a flak jacket, helmet, bedding, and a MOPP suit.

I ask, "What about ammo?"

He points off to his right, at another container twenty yards away. It sits alone in a hole like this one, but it's surrounded by sandbags and concertina wire. "That's the armory."

I take the platoon over and find inside the hatch a corporal at the same type of desk as the supply NCO. Behind him sits a staff sergeant with ammo crates for a field desk. A Marine guard with a loaded M-16 is behind the two of them.

I'm told each man must register his weapon, including my .45, and I'm given forms for the platoon. Passing them around, I tell everyone what's expected. "Name, rank, and rifle number. Sign the bottom." I give the completed forms back to the corporal, and he begins handing out the ammunition. Each Marine receives eight boxes of 5.56 and eight magazines. Each box has twenty rounds. Staff Sergeant Woods checks out a .45 with ammo.

Behind the staff sergeant stand two racks of M-16 rifles. I ask, "Can I check out a rifle for myself, Corporal?"

He looks behind at the staff sergeant, who stands and moves forward. "We're not supposed to issue above the rank of sergeant."

"I'm going to be running convoys to Jabar until we invade Kuwait. I could use a little more firepower."

He stares at me for a moment then tells the corporal, "Issue him one." Turning back to his desk, he says, "I'm not sure how long you'll be able to keep it, Staff Sergeant."

"Understood."

With ammunition for all our weapons in hand, we head to our tent. Inside, the men start going through the MREs for breakfast. I pick out spaghetti with meat sauce, one of my favorites, and sit next to Woods, who's eating what looks like beef stew. I watch as he pours the entire tiny bottle of hot sauce on his meal. That bottle is something these guys would kill for. Just like in 'Nam, if you can change the taste of what you're eating, it's a good thing.

I tell Woody, "As soon as we're done here, take the platoon over to the motor pool. I'll meet you there after I talk with Howard."

"Copy that."

At the Motor T tent, I walk in and find the master sergeant sitting behind a green field desk. To his left is a board covered in a plastic film with a listing of the company vehicles. This explains what is available, what has been issued, and to whom. Each vehicle has a date it was signed out and, in some cases, an expected return date. My eyes center on the Dragons and the wrecker. One thing absent from the available list is Hummers. The few on the board have all been taken by upper staff NCOs and officers, with no return dates listed.

"You get everything you need from Supply?" Master Sergeant Howard asks.

"Yes, we did, Master Sergeant. Was that a MOPP one alert earlier?"

"No need for the formalities, Green. Call me Top. And no, MOPP zero. That's a long burst followed by a short. MOPP one is a continuous short burst. We're in a perpetual state of MOPP zero, so make sure your people keep their suits close by."

I nod. Top lays out the plan. "The captain wants you to take the convoy to Jabar tomorrow. We don't have any extra Hummers, so you'll have to double up as an A driver. Hopefully some Hummers will show up on the dock soon and you'll get your own. Then you won't have to go as an assistant driver anymore."

"I noticed there are women in the platoon. How many are drivers?" I ask.

"We have six women drivers and two mechanics. There's Women Marines belonging to different platoons in the company as well. They're all billeted together outside of our area. If for any reason you need to go there, don't just barge into their tent. You must announce who you are and who you want to see. Staff Sergeant Matters is in command of the women. Between you and me, she wouldn't be here if it wasn't for the women drivers, who we need to meet our numbers. Don't get me wrong, she knows her stuff, it's just the battalion XO does not take kindly to women in a combat area."

I have my own thoughts on this, but I stay silent until I know how this is going to play out. "How many vehicles are going tomorrow?"

"Are all your drivers HET licensed? I'll need to see all licenses so they can be logged."

"Yes. Our I and I made sure of it months ago. I'll get them for you. So we'll be taking Dragons to Jabar?"

"Yes. You'll be picking up ISO containers. But you're to bring back any vehicles placard for the battalion. Make sure everyone going is licensed. You know your people, and I'll give you a list of licensed drivers from Eighth Engines. Any of your mechanics licensed to drive an LSVR?"

"Yes, we have two. Are we expecting a Dragon wrecker?"

"Affirmative, and the captain wants it here, so make it a priority."

"Copy that. Only taking those six Dragons, then?"

"Yes. In the morning, I'll give you a list of what we're expecting. You'll have to search the dock and find what's ours. Get the ISO containers first and then look for the wrecker and whatever else you can find. This is only the beginning of your treks back to the port."

"Copy that." By his leave, I walk out of the tent and head to the motor pool. Staff Sergeant Woods has our Marines in a ragged formation. The other men and women stand around.

PFC Tilly asks, "We going on a convoy tomorrow, Staff Sergeant? Are we all going?"

"I need twelve drivers, all HET licensed, including me."

Speaking quietly, Woody asks, "You going to drive? Is that smart?"

"Yeah, Woody, I have to. There are no Hummers available, and I need to drive something back from the docks." Turning away from him, I say, "Sergeant Ford. Collect all the military driving licenses from the people who came in last night and get them over to Top Howard."

"Copy that, Staff."

I call Sergeant Brown and Staff Sergeant Matters to have their Marines fall in, then I explain what will be happening tomorrow. "We'll be picking up six ISOs. That's job one. I need a wrecker driver for tomorrow. We'll be looking for an LSVR. That's job two. Job three will be any vehicles placard Sixth Engineers or Eighth Engineers. I'll need a name on the wrecker driver, Staff Sergeant Woods."

"Copy that. Corporal Baker, that's you."

Baker gives a smile and a thumbs-up.

"Anything else you need from me?"

"Negative. You can take your mechanics." To the platoon, I say, "Corporal Baker, you stay here." Woods takes his mechanics from the platoon and heads over to his lightweight maintenance tent.

"Sergeant Brown, I'll need four of your drivers. All have to be HET licensed." Needing a sergeant to go along with me tomorrow, I ask Brown first. "Sergeant Brown, are you HET licensed?"

"Negative, Staff." No need to say anything more. I know my sergeant tomorrow will be Ford.

"Staff Sergeant Matters, I'll need two of your Marines as well, again HET licensed. The Marines you both pick, along with those I choose, will meet here at seventeen hundred hours. Any questions?" There are none. "Chow goes in an hour. Anyone wanting to walk the twenty-minute hike for a hot meal, you're welcome to do so. That's all for now. Dismissed."

At the 1700-hour formation, I explain what will be expected tomorrow, going over a few convoy regulations and assuring them we'll maintain discipline. I let everyone know there will be civilians out there with weapons, reminding them to stay clear and remain alert.

Before the formation ends, I say, "Sergeant Ford, I need you to put the HETs in convoy order tonight. I want the drivers and their As performing PMs on their vehicles as well. Be sure you're all topped off on fuel. Any driver needing fuel, Sergeant Brown can tell you where the Farm is."

Later that night, I'm back in the tent and cleaning my weapon while listening to the laughter and watching the horseplay getting out of hand. I wait for Sergeant Ford to say something. I want him to be in control of this tent, not me. The last thing I need is to change my relationship with these men. Billeting with them puts me in a situation of becoming their friend. I need to keep my distance. Friendship is not the way to command Marines, especially in combat.

Trying to ignore what's going on, I take two magazines, fully loaded, and tape them together with black electrical tape, one upside down from the other, a trick I learned in 'Nam. Now if a firefight erupts, I can easily unload one and quickly reload the weapon, just like in Vietnam.

PFC Tilly watches me with interest until I finish. "Why did you do that, Staff Sergeant?"

While putting my rifle back together, I answer, "When I was in 'Nam, my first patrol, we run into an enemy base camp. When the shooting started and my first mag ran out"—I slowly demonstrate—"I simply turn it over and pop in a full metal jacket. I'm ready to go." I look up at the young Marine and see myself, twenty years ago. "You should do the same thing, PFC. You have any tape?"

"Negative, Staff."

"It's a good thing I packed extra tape from home." I hand him my roll, and he grabs two magazines and starts taping. Others in the platoon see what's going on, and before long, the horseplay ends and everyone is taping their magazines together. Now these Marines are getting ready for war, not a game. I'll talk to Sergeant

Ford tomorrow about the tent activities and keeping the men ready. For now, it's lights out and time to sleep. Tomorrow will come early enough, and we'll be on the road at first light. My job is to make sure we're ready for whatever is out there.

CHAPTER 19

THE ROAD

9 January 1991

A HAND TOUCHES MY SHOULDER, SNAPPING me alert. Fist clenched, I'm ready to strike whoever it is.

"Easy, Staff Sergeant," someone mutters while stepping back. "I'm Corporal Philips. Duty NCO. It's zero five hundred."

"Sorry, Corporal. Next time, call me, from over there." I point at the tent flap several feet away.

He looks over at the hatchway and says, "Next time, I'll send someone else to wake you. From over there."

The duty walks out, and I sit up, my feet touching down on the cold desert ground. My trousers still on from the night before, I finish dressing and step outside.

Geez, it's cold. Feels more like the Midwest than Saudi Arabia.

Early morning light filters through the dark. There in the motor pool are six Dragons, all lined up and ready to go. Light escaping through the cracks in the Motor T office hatch indicates someone is in there. Inside I find Top Howard and Sergeant Brown sharing what smells like coffee. A tiny propane stove heats the treat.

"Good morning, Top. Can I get a cup of that?"

"Sure, Green," the master sergeant answers. "Good job having those trucks ready to go first thing this morning. You going to be ready to haul ass?"

"I'll let the troops sleep until zero five thirty. We'll be on the road by sunup."

I pour hot coffee into a borrowed cup and sip the brew. Master

Sergeant Howard provides some final details on my mission. "Here's the paperwork for the ISOs, Staff Sergeant. Remember, anything you find placard for our battalions will be brought here ASAP. Make sure you write down what gear you find but can't bring back on this run. The captain will want to know what's still out there."

The master sergeant sits down behind his green desk. "Do you know Master Sergeant Belinsky, from Water Platoon?"

"Yes, I do."

"He says there's a reverse osmosis water purifying machine on the dock. It's priority. It's placard Engineer Support Company Sixth Engineer Battalion. He knows this because he's the one who placarded the machine. Find it. Load it on one of the HETs. And bring it back."

"Copy that." Setting down the empty coffee cup, I add, "Almost time to get my drivers up. Sergeant Brown, wake the four drivers from your platoon. Have them in formation by zero six hundred."

With a mouthful of coffee, Brown offers his cup up like a toast to signify he will. I leave the office and walk to my tent. Inside, I go find Sergeant Ford. "Ford, get up. Get the drivers going and on the road."

His eyes still heavy with sleep, he answers, "Copy that, Staff."

By zero six hundred, the Marines are in formation. I call them to attention then put them at ease. "Listen up. You have twenty-five minutes to get your gear together and be at your assigned vehicles. Bring one MRE. We will not be back for noon chow. If you want pogey bait, bring it. Bring all the ammunition you have. I'll be in the lead truck and Sergeant Ford in the last. There are no radios, so we'll communicate using our headlights. Lance Corporal Kelly."

"Yes, Staff Sergeant."

"You're in number two position. If you see my hazards flashing, put yours on. Each vehicle behind you will do the same. Flashers mean trouble ahead. Stay alert and follow my vehicle. Does anyone have a question?"

No one does.

"This is not the best possible means of communicating, but

it's all we've got. I want the convoy spacing no more than three truck lengths. Our top speed will be forty-five miles per hour. Stay alert of the vehicle ahead of you. If you get separated from the convoy, try to stay on the road until we can all pull off. I've heard the Arab truck drivers out there are crazy SOBs, so watch out for that. Highway 95 or Abu Haidriyah Highway is our road to Jabar. Everyone write it down." I stall for a minute, allowing anyone who might have a question to ask, but no one does. "Okay, let's saddle up."

By 0630, the drivers are all in their vehicles. I stand outside and look up and down the row of HET Dragons, assuring we're ready. Once we're good to go, I climb into the passenger side and tell my driver, "Let's go, PFC."

The convoy passes through the gate we came through two nights ago and back on the sand road, which is bumpy as hell. We're making good time. But if it weren't for our seat belts, we'd be bouncing off the roof of our tractor. "Slow down a little, PFC. I don't want anyone to break something." Using the side mirror, I keep the convoy in sight.

While reading a hand-drawn map in the notes Top had given me, Tilly shouts with excitement, "Hard surface road ahead, Staff Sergeant."

I look up and see the highway. "That's our way, PFC."

Highway 95 to Al Jabar Port is uneventful for the first few miles. It's a two-lane road, and the traffic is light. We pass the point where our bus entered 95 after leaving the airport on our way to Mishab two days ago. A short distance later, 95 becomes a four-lane highway. Almost immediately, the surface changes. The HET's tires cross over huge ruts in the road, causing Tilly to almost lose control. In my mirror, I can see the Dragons behind me violently swerving from side to side as the convoy struggles to keep them on the road.

My eyes open wide as the young PFC fights to regain control. The truck is tossed about like a rag doll until finally we're back on the road, our tires riding between the ruts. I ask, "You got this?"

"Yes, Staff Sergeant. I'm going to stay out of those ruts. You drive over them, and the Dragon jumps and pulls like crazy."

"Look at the size of those grooves. Where the hell did they come from?"

"I don't know."

Driving between the ruts allows Tilly to maintain control, but it puts us out of our lane and into traffic that wants to pass on our left.

"What the fuck. You see that, Staff?" Tilly cries out as a Saudi truck, driving in the ruts, passes so close to us, our mirrors almost touch.

He's riding in the groove. And he has control. That's how you drive this damn road. "Get in the grooves, Tilly. If you stay in 'em, you'll be okay."

"I don't think so. If I cross them, I'll lose control."

"Do it! If you don't, the next truck will come by and take your door off."

Tilly looks at me for a second, wrinkles his brow, and allows the Dragon to cross the channel. The tires pull as they fight to stay out. The bouncing truck throws us both hard against our seat belts. Finally, the truck is in the grooves and running smooth.

After a Saudi truck flies past, I realize where those ruts come from.

"They're hauling a lot of weight. I don't think they have weight limits in this country. You see all the wheels on that sumbitch, plus the extra weight over his tandems. That's why those ruts are so freaking deep. Those trucks made 'em."

The traffic on this highway continues to move in a reckless manner. Each time a truck passes us, only inches separate our vehicles from theirs. I keep my eye out for Sergeant Ford's number six Dragon, and when I see it, I know we're still good to go.

Along the side of the road sits something peculiar—very expensive automobiles. No one is with them.

"You see those cars, Tilly?"

"Yeah, Staff Sergeant, I do. Very expensive."

Still looking out my window, I say, "Yeah, there's a Mercedes-

Benz and a Ferrari." My head snaps as I follow something I can't believe. "Shit, man, that was a Rolls-Royce. I think it's abandoned."

Settling back in my seat, I explain, "Coming out here, I heard the Saudis don't have to work at menial labor jobs. Their government brings in foreign workers to do that. Every citizen gets oil money from the king. I bet they leave those cars there, abandon them, then go buy new ones."

"Really? You think so?" Tilly asks.

"Hell, I don't know, maybe."

The stress of driving over this road can take a physical and mental toll on my Marines. If they wander only a few inches, the drivers can lose control. I need to give them a break.

Up ahead on our left, several trucks and autos are parked in front of a large one-story building. "Looks like a truck stop, Tilly. Put on your turn signal. Pull in and stop along the road."

PFC Tilly executes my order and comes to a stop along the edge of the highway.

The other five trucks follow us off, and I watch in my mirror until all the Dragons stop in a row. I exit my vehicle and check the line. Once I'm satisfied we're secure, I tell the drivers to exit their vehicles. As soon as everyone's together, I give a briefing. "Everyone carries their weapon inside. Check your vehicles before you go in. Make sure nothing is broken. Pound your tires for flats. I need two volunteers to do a walking guard around our trucks."

Two lance corporals from Eighth Engineers volunteer.

Inside the building are Arabs with automatic weapons. Some are slung over the shoulder while others carry them in their hands. As we walk past, they smile, and I reply with the same. In the center of this establishment is a long counter. Behind it are several employees selling books, drinks, and food. A delicious aroma grabs my attention. I look left toward the smell, and twenty feet away, whole chickens are roasting over an open flame. I walk over to investigate and find in addition to the chicken some strips of beef on a grill. Though it's still morning, my appetite is winning this battle.

This is so good. I've got to get some. This beats the hell out of my MRE.

Before any of us can indulge, we need to find a place to piss.

After several minutes of walking around, I find what the Arabs consider a bathroom. The building is in the back, outside the main shop. After entering through an open doorway, we find a ten-by-ten-foot structure. Inside, I can't believe what I see. There are no flush toilets, only a cement trench running around the wall of the whole building. I watch as men stand and urinate into this channel. The liquid runs to a single corner then outside onto the ground. With little ventilation, the smell is horrendous.

At the trench, I prepare to relieve myself. *So this is a third-world pisser. Hell, their country, their way.* I expel my urine into the trench.

Walking back to the building, I notice farther back in another lot are diesel pumps, and a few Arab trucks are fueling.

I approach two Marines from Sixth Engines who are buying something from the counter. "As soon as you're done, relieve those guards outside." They acknowledge my order.

Some of the Marines are buying candy and American cigarettes. It seems American money is very welcome here. At the counter with the chickens, I point and ask, "How much for a chicken?"

The Arab smiles. "Five dollar US."

I take out my wallet and hand him a five-dollar bill. He wraps the chicken in brown paper and puts it in a bag. I motion to a familiar can of Coca-Cola. "One dollar US," he tells me. After I give him another dollar, he hands me the soda. The colors of the pop can are those of Coke, but the words on the opposite side of the can are not in English but Arabic. I buy a second can to take back to Mishab.

From behind me, a Marine asks, "Staff Sergeant, can we make phone calls?" It's Corporal Baker, the wrecker driver.

"Where do they have these phones, Baker?"

"Over here, Staff." He leads me to the back of the store. Along a rear wall are six pay phones, just like back in the States. I know how badly these men want to talk with someone back home, but not now. "Maybe on the way back, Corporal. First thing we need to do is pick up our gear. We'll have more time on our return to Mishab."

At the food counter, Sergeant Ford is buying a chicken.

"Sergeant Ford."

He faces me and responds, "Yeah, Staff."

"Let's get everybody back to the convoy. We need to get to the port, ASAP."

"Copy that," he says as he receives his chicken. Over at another counter, I spot the two Women Marine drivers buying pogey bait. Candy and soda is on their list. I walk over to talk with them, something I should have done earlier.

One WM is a lance corporal and the other a PFC. They're both so young and easy on the eyes. They look like children, and the thought of them being in harm's way disturbs me. I immediately put out of my head any thoughts of protecting them more than any other Marine. My job is to treat them as the Marines they are. I guess I'm just old-school.

"How are you two doing?" I ask.

"Good, Staff Sergeant," the lance corporal answers.

"We have to be going, so get your pogey and back to your truck." There are no names on our desert uniforms, so I ask, "Which one of you is Underwood?"

"I am, Staff Sergeant."

Both girls are less than five seven, and Underwood reminds me of my daughter with her blond hair and brown eyes.

"How are you finding it out there? Can you handle that road?"

"Yes. I get tossed around, but we're good to go. No worse than the guys."

With a smile, I realize I've been reminded to treat her not as a woman but as a Marine.

Still, all I see is a teenage girl with a loaded M-16. "All right, back to your vehicle. We need to get moving." Turning from the girls, I call out, "Sergeant Ford, get everyone back to their vehicles!"

We're on the road at 1000 hours. The traffic to the port increases as we get closer. I swear the chances for death on this road are as dangerous as any firefight I've been in. We enter an area crowded with buildings and structures reminding me of an industrial complex. Proceeding down the road, I see an oil rig with men working on it.

Looking for oil.

Across an open field are some large pumps. I say to PFC Tilly, "See those pumps there? Think that's for oil?"

To my surprise, the young Marine tells me what they are. "That's a Nodding Donkey."

Surprised, I ask, "What's a … what did you call it? A Nodding Donkey?"

"Yes. It pumps up oil from deep underground."

"How do you know this?"

"I'm from Texas, Staff. My dad works on oil rigs and pumps like that. He'd sometimes take me with him, and I'd watch him work."

"Really. So where does the oil go after it's pumped up?"

Tilly looks to his left, then with eyes on the road, he says, "I don't see any holding tanks, so there must be a pipeline under the rigs. The oil and water is pumped into a pipeline then heads off to some holding tank, far away."

Looking straight at the PFC, I feel a little awkward that this young Marine knows more than me, but at the same time, I'm amazed. "Oil and water?"

"Yeah, after the initial strike, water mixes with the oil deep underground. It's separated at the refinery. That's how we do it back in Texas."

Tilly keeps his eyes straight ahead. His face shows no emotion when he asks me a question I've heard before. "Staff Sergeant, do you think that's what this war is about?" He looks at me. "Are we risking our lives for oil?"

I give it a moment before I answer. What do I say to this kid? Whatever I say, I know it'll get back to the whole platoon. "Here's what I know, PFC. Iraq invaded that country, probably for the oil. But whatever the reason, it shouldn't be allowed. If we don't stop them here, then we'll have to stop them somewhere else." I shuffle in my seat, pull the seat belt loose from my chest, then say,

"One thing's for sure, Marine. We don't choose the wars. We just fight them."

I'm alerted to an overhead sign. "That's where we're going, Tilly. Follow those arrows."

"But the sign is in Arabic."

"The words *Al Jabar* are at the bottom. That has to be the port. Follow that sign."

"Copy that."

When we arrive at the port entranceway, we're stopped by two Marine Corps MPs and two Saudi Arabian soldiers. I hand my paperwork to a Marine Corps sergeant. After checking it over, he hands the papers back and gives me instructions. "Stay on the road, and the docks are ahead. They'll be to your left, about a half mile or so."

"Copy that."

After he waves us through, I look over at Tilly. "We made it. We're here."

CHAPTER 20

THE PORT

10 January 1991

I TAKE THE CONVOY DOWN THE road, searching for the docks. Even though all the signs are in Arabic, I don't think I'll get lost. White single-story buildings are on both sides of the road. I have no idea what they're used for. I keep the convoy moving while I look for the dock. In the distance, above the tops of the buildings, I see the bridge of a cargo ship. Now I know we're close.

The street turns left and ends at a T in the road. Across the intersection is the dock and, beyond that, the water. "This has got to be what we're looking for, PFC."

"Which way?" Tilly asks.

"Turn right, toward the ship."

We get an awesome view of this huge boat. The bridge I saw over the top of those buildings is at the rear of this vessel. At the front are tall beams I guess are masts. I've never been this close to a cargo ship before. It looks so big, and we're still several hundred yards away.

On my left is the dock, filled with everything an army needs to fight. Amazed, Tilly says, "Look at all this stuff, Staff Sergeant."

My eyes glance down the dock and on the ship. It's off-loading ISO containers. Needing to find a certain piece of equipment, I say, "Hey, slow down." As I stare out Tilly's window, the young Marine asks, "What you looking for, Staff Sergeant?"

"I need to find that osmosis machine." Moments later, I say,

"There it is. That's it." I sit back in my seat and make a mental note of the location.

As we continue toward the ship, on my left I spot the ISO containers. They're stacked one on top of another in a group between the Hummers and the front-end loaders. "Stop here, PFC," I command.

Tilly presses hard on the brakes, causing me to brace myself against the dashboard. Out of my truck, I call Sergeant Ford over and tell him, "I'm going to find a container handler to load up these boxes. Find as many ISO placards as you can for sixth or eighth battalions. Be ready to load when I get back."

"Copy that."

"Don't forget to track down our Dragons and any vehicles belonging to our battalion. Make notes."

He confirms with a nod.

While Sergeant Ford looks for our equipment, I walk down the dock toward the liner. I stop at the edge of the ship's berth and watch as a Rough Terrain Container Handler heads up the ramp of the ship. A second RTCH is on the ship with an Intermodal Container, waiting for the ramp to clear. A Marine talking into a headset seems to be in charge.

I tap him on the shoulder. "By your leave."

He turns and greets me, and I see his rank. "Excuse me, Master Sergeant."

He removes his headset. "What is it, Staff Sergeant?"

"I came from Mishab to pick up gear."

He motions me to follow him to a quieter area. Once there, he asks, "What's your unit?"

I hand him my paperwork and answer, "Both the Sixth and Eighth Engineer Battalions. My priorities are ISO containers, one Dragon wrecker, and a reverse osmosis."

"How many trucks do you have?"

"I came down with six, but I have enough drivers to go back with twelve."

"I'll send a handler down as soon as I can. He'll verify what you're taking and sign off on your orders. In the meantime, find your other vehicles so when he arrives, your convoy will be up and ready for loading."

"Copy that." Taking back my paperwork, I ask, "I spotted the reverse osmosis in line while I was pulling in. Do you have any tie-downs? We had none back at Mishab."

"I'll make sure the handler has some with him."

Finding what is ours is a massive job. There's no unit order to the staging. The only good thing is, the equipment types are all together.

Hours pass, and it's almost 1500 hours when the container handler arrives. The last three HETs fall in line behind the six I brought down. Behind them are a five-ton troop carrier and the wrecker we needed. We're good to go.

A young lance corporal driving the handler asks, "You in charge, Staff Sergeant?"

"Yep. I have eight ISO containers and a reverse osmosis machine to load on the HET flatbeds. Can you load the osmosis too?"

"Negative. I'll get you a forklift." He picks up a radio handset and talks with someone on the dock. "They'll be here ASAP."

The RTCH is loading the containers when the forklift arrives. I climb up the side to talk with the operator. "I have a reverse osmosis a hundred yards down the line. I left a Marine there to identify it for you. Do you have the tie-downs?"

"Do you have paperwork?" he challenges.

I let his attitude slide and show him what I have. "You can see there"—I point at what is written on the forms—"all the serial numbers are correct." Then, with an attitude of my own, I add, "You can climb down and check those out yourself, Private."

He nods and reaches to the floor on his right, pulling up three tie-down straps. I give him a smile and a thumbs-up, saying, "I'll send a Dragon down to you. Give the driver the straps." I jump down, and the forklift is off. Walking down the line, I order the last HET in the convoy to follow the forklift.

I take a deep breath, hold it a moment, then exhale a rush of air. Everything is good to go.

Checking the time, I see it's 1530. I take one last look around and spot something that stops me cold. There on the dock is something I had forgotten about, an M123 ten-ton tractor sitting among a group of Low Boy trailers. This is the same type of vehicle I drove back in Indiana for the company.

It almost looks like my truck. Shit, that is my truck!

I run to the vehicle and read the placard: "Sixth Engineers Support Battalion." I'm excited. I found my tractor. With nothing to drive and since I'm the only one licensed for this particular vehicle, it's mine to take back to Mishab.

It's 1600 hours, and the convoy is finally ready to head back. I tell Ford, "I don't want to be out after dark. We need to haul ass. Get everybody together. I'll pass final orders."

I turn to Tilly and ask, "Can you lead this convoy back to Mishab?"

Hesitating, he answers, "Yes, I think so."

"No 'think so,' PFC. Either you can or you cannot. Which is it?"

He thrusts his shoulders back and has a gleam in his eye. "Yes, I can lead the convoy back."

Tilly is one of my weaker Marines, and I hope that assigning him this task will give him some much-needed self-confidence. I don't have to worry about which way he goes, because I'll be right behind him.

I give the final orders. "PFC Tilly is lead truck. I'll be number two. Sergeant Ford is number eleven, and the wrecker is tail end. Does anyone have a question?"

Corporal Baker asks, "Can we stop and make phone calls?"

"No. There's no time. We'll find time tomorrow. This trip, we keep going until we're back at Mishab. Mount up. Let's get on the road."

The trip to Mishab is as dangerous in the late afternoon as it was in the morning. More than once, a vehicle in my convoy has its mirror rubbed by an aggressive Arab truck driver. The size of our convoy slows our return. The lack of communications is something I need to address before I take out any more convoys. But that's for later. Right now, I need to be cautious.

As the sun sets over the desert road, we drive through the gate of Mishab and into the Motor T yard. The captain stands waiting outside the Motor T office. I stop my truck in front of it and climb out to meet him.

He says, "I was getting worried."

"Yes, sir." I hand him the paperwork. "Here's a list of equipment we brought back and what's still at Mishab. There could be more than this, but it's all we found. They were still unloading ships." The captain takes the paperwork, and I add, "We have Water Platoon's reverse osmosis, Captain." I point at the truck hauling the machine as it enters the Motor T yard. "With your permission, sir, I need to get a forklift from Heavy Equipment. I want the osmosis off-loaded at Water Platoon ASAP. I'm sure Master Sergeant Belinsky wants to start making clean water as soon as possible."

The captain smiles and nods as he continues to examine the paperwork.

"I'll be right back, sir." I run to catch up to the truck hauling the reverse osmosis. Hopping onto the driver's-side floorboard, I ask the operator, "Do you know where Water Platoon is?"

"Affirmative, Staff Sergeant."

"Take this vehicle to their lot. Get the tie-downs off the osmosis and wait for the forklift. I want this thing off tonight. When you're done, take the truck back to the yard and do your post OP. Don't worry about fuel tonight. The Farm closed after dark."

"Copy that, Staff Sergeant."

After hopping down from the Dragon, I walk to my truck and drive it into the Motor T yard. I park and get the Marines together for some final orders. "Everyone does a post OP on their vehicle before you do anything else. Make sure you're ready to go in the morning. The truck you drove in on will be your vehicle until further notice. When we go out tomorrow morning, if your truck's assigned, then so are you. Any questions?"

"Should we fuel up, Staff Sergeant?" Corporal Baker asks.

"Negative. The Farm's closed. We'll fuel in the morning. Anybody else?"

There are no more questions, so I dismiss the troops and walk over to the Motor T office. I report in to Master Sergeant Howard.

"I need a forklift sent to Water Platoon, Top. I'd like the reverse osmosis off-loaded tonight." Howard picks up the receiver of a landline and makes the call.

After I pass along to the master sergeant what happened today, I return to the ten-ton and do my own post OP. Most of the troops are back in their tent and probably chowing down. When I'm done, I'll head there myself and eat that chicken and drink my Coke. Then, I'll get some sleep.

We have no idea when the war is going to start, but I know we have to be ready when it does. That means everything has to be back from Al-Jabar.

In the morning, the captain pulls me aside to explain some changes he's made. "The list you gave me of what's still on the dock isn't everything this battalion is expecting. You said you saw more ships. Our gear should be on them. I want you to take more drivers with you, including the women. I want as many vehicles as possible back here ASAP. I've assigned a five-ton to your convoy to carry those extra drivers. Take the HETs down. Load ISOs and cargo on them. I don't know how much time we have before this whole thing gets real. We need to move this along."

"Aye, aye, sir. I need communications for my trucks. Can we get radios?"

"Affirmative. I put in an emergency requisition for three Prick radios last night. Second Force Service Support Group Communications Company arrived two days ago. There are no more radio shortages."

"Are we picking up gear for the FSSG too, sir?"

"Negative. Last night, Sixth Motor Transport Battalion rolled in. They'll start sending out convoys as soon as they're organized. How soon can you be on the road?"

"We'll stop at the fuel farm on our way out. About two hours. But I need those radios, sir."

"I'll make a call and have them delivered to you at the Farm. You need to go now."

"Copy that."

As soon as the convoy forms, I take it to the fuel farm. This place is huge. There are giant black fuel bladders, hundreds of square feet in size. They sit inside dugout areas with berm walls around them. They're so huge they dwarf a man standing next to them. The place is being guarded like an ammo dump. MPs are at the gates, and they have walking patrols. Concertina wire surrounds the whole place. Bulk Fuel Marines tend to the bladders and fuel our trucks. The radios show up, and after two hours, we're on our way.

Along the way, we take breaks at the truck stop on Highway 95. While there, I allow the troops to make their phone calls home. I warn them, "We don't need to worry anyone. Don't talk about what we're doing or the Arab drivers we're dealing with. Keep your conversations specific to family."

I don't worry about anyone saying anything about the upcoming invasion. None of us know a thing about it. I add, "Don't try to talk about what you don't know. The folks back home know more than we do."

16 January 1991

Last night was the end of a rough convoy. It started when I took the fleet to view a Dragon wreck in the combat deadline lot. The truck hit an Arab semi head-on. The steering wheel was out the back window, and bloodstains were everywhere. The driver was DOA. "Remember, people, this Marine is dead, and he doesn't even get a Purple Heart. Stay alert out there. So far we've been lucky, but that can change at any time." The troops look concerned but ready to get back on the road.

The ride down is better these days. The drivers have all learned how to handle the Arabs we share this road with. At the dock, we find a long line backed up from every unit in FSSG picking up their respective equipment. It's so clustered today we wait three hours before we're able to check for our gear. The dock that was once loaded with hundreds of military trucks, heavy equipment, and generators is almost empty now. It turns out the only thing left to pick up is a Hummer. The wrecker tows it back because it's dead-lined. It's missing a steering wheel, a door, and all its windshields. It belongs to Eighth Engines. At least it wasn't the reserves from Indiana who sent down this piece of junk. The extra time there has us getting back at 2100. Driving the last few miles in total darkness is not a good thing. The roads are bad enough in the daylight, but after dark, they're treacherous.

17 January 1991

It's 0330. I should be asleep, but my Chicago Bulls are making a run for the NBA title. They're up by five in the fourth quarter. Without warning, the radio goes silent. I shout, "I lost the game! Now what?"

Then comes the news we've been waiting for. "We interrupt this broadcast for a special bulletin. Moments ago, coalition forces began launching air strikes against Iraq. Hundreds of aircraft from the United States, Great Britain, Saudi Arabia, and other coalition nations began their attack at three thirty a.m. Baghdad time. The attacks began with cruise missiles fired from US ships in the Persian Gulf. Now, John Holliman, located at a hotel in the Iraqi capital."

"Thank you, Tom. Moments ago, the skies above Baghdad lit up after air raid sirens sounded across the city. You can hear the antiaircraft guns firing. I do not see any coalition aircraft in the sky, but I do see and hear explosions happening on the outskirts and in the downtown area. The war to drive Saddam Hussein out of Kuwait has begun. Desert Storm is under way."

Holy shit!

In a loud voice, I ask those in my tent, "Hey, you guys, anyone awake?"

"Yeah, Staff Sergeant, I hear it too," one of them says.

From across the tent, the Marines are waking to the news the war has started. When one Marine says, "It's all different now. This is real," I glance at my watch, and it's 0345.

Negotiations are over. From now on, my Marines and I will be in harm's way.

CHAPTER 21

IRAQ FIGHTS BACK

18 January 1991

ONVOYS THAT WERE SET TO leave for Mishab today are on standby. Major Shepard, our company commander, has called all the senior personnel to a meeting. I show up at the major's tent with Staff Sergeant Woods and Staff Sergeant Matters. This is the first time I've been in the major's tent. This is a huge tent normally accommodating up to twenty or more Marines. The captain has put the extra space to good use. The tent is in two sections. The first, closest to the hatch, is set aside for logistics. In the middle sits a table covered with a large map that I recognize as Mishab and its surrounding area. A large pin board stands to the left, and on it are lists of platoons. Among the lists is Motor Transport. As I strain to read the names, I see the chain of command. The captain is first, Top is next, and then me.

I guess it means I'm third in charge. Cool.

On the right side of the room are two computers, lit up and active, resting on a long bench about three feet high.

Behind the logistics area are racks with bedding and individual gear on top. It's obvious the XO, first sergeant, and all the company platoon commanders are staying here.

The major is sitting on the rack closest to the logistics area. It crosses my mind how all those in charge of our company are together in one tent.

Why would they do that? The whole command together makes

for a special target. If an enemy rocket or artillery round hits this tent, Master Sergeant Howard and I are in charge.

As soon as the major receives the word everyone is present, he stands and moves forward to the table. "There are two matters I need to discuss with you all tonight. Most of you are already aware that to our front is a company from the Twenty-Sixth Marines. They are Charlie Company, a reserve unit. They are what stand between Mishab and ... an Iraqi ground assault."

Leaning over to Woody, I whisper, "I hope they have more than a hundred twenty rounds a man." He smiles.

The major begins. "The air campaign is happening for one reason, to have a successful ground campaign. When the invasion begins, certain elements of the company will move forward. They'll be in direct support of combat forces. The XO will be in command there, and I will be in command here. This is the way General Krulak wants it. This unit will be part of battalion forward. As the grunts and armor advance, so will they." The major takes a few seconds to make eye contact. "Motor Transport Platoon will follow immediately with supplies for battalion forward. Staff Sergeant Green."

I stand. "Yes, sir," I say, surprised he knows my name.

"You will be taking all convoys forward."

"Copy that, sir."

"Master Sergeant Balister."

"Yes, sir."

"Your road graders will flatten the road following the tank assault. I will notify the rest of you what your role will be during the invasion. I can promise you this, everyone here will see action. Does anyone have a question?"

A gunnery sergeant I have not seen before asks, "Why the company of Marines to our front, sir?"

The major stares at the gunny, and I have the feeling this is a question he doesn't want to answer. "All friendly combat forces are to our rear. We're the closest battalion to the Iraqi lines."

Such disturbing news has everyone looking and mumbling.

How the hell does that make sense?

The major continues, "Keep this information to yourselves. I don't want this news spread around to the troops."

Trips to Al Jabar Port become our daily routine. In between convoys, I make sure the trucks have their preventive maintenance completed. The sirens that sound a warning of a chemical or biological attack have us all on edge. Every time they go off, we rush to put on our MOPP suits. The problem is, they're false alarms. The alerts are having a reverse effect on my Marines and me. Every time we're told to run to our MOPP suits, we move a little slower. We all want the ground war to start. The days have become long and boring, and anticipation of the upcoming battle has us all ready and good to go.

Since the meeting with the company CO, we've had no more information about what's going on outside of Mishab. Since the air war started, phone calls back home are no longer allowed. If we stop at the truck stop, it's for a head call or pogey bait.

21 January 1991

Today has a small convoy going to Mishab, only four HETS. Sergeant Ford and I are putting together the driver assignments outside the tent. Staff Sergeant Matters walks up and tells me, "The captain wants you in the office, Green."

"Do you know why?"

"Negative," she says.

"Copy that." Before I leave, I remind Ford, "Make sure everyone has an MRE and full canteens."

He gives me a thumbs-up.

I walk into the office and report in.

"Staff Sergeant, you know you will be my convoy commander when the shit hits the fan?"

"Yes, sir. I do."

"When things get real, you're going to need your own Hummer."

"I didn't think there were any Hummers out there, sir."

"There aren't. I'm yanking one from a master sergeant in

headquarters. He's not happy, but that's the way it is. Pick it up today. You can start using it immediately. The master sergeant's name is Quince." He hands me a piece of paper. "These are the vehicle ID numbers."

I try to hide my excitement. Christmas isn't allowed in this country, but this sure feels like it. I go back to the yard and have Ford grab a five-ton to take me to headquarters. A Hummer parked outside has the matching number I'm looking for.

"Hell, Staff Sergeant, just take it," Ford grunts.

"Negative. I'll go in and find the master sergeant and tell him I'm taking the Hummer."

I walk into headquarters and find the master sergeant sitting down with other E-8s. Seeing me, he scowls and grabs the paperwork from my hand, but otherwise he doesn't give me a hard time. That's a load off my mind. I drive the Hummer back to the yard and decide right then to name this truck. The ground war hasn't started, and this war could go on for months. This could be my vehicle for the duration, and I want to make it mine.

I paint "CJ" on the side panel above the tier. Then I harden the floor with sandbags to prevent shrapnel from coming through, a technique I learned in Vietnam.

I use CJ that very day to drive to the port. The ride there is much more comfortable than the HETS, and Ford, my A driver, is happy about that.

22 January 1991

Six days into the air campaign, we learn from Armed Forces Radio that Saddam Hussein orders the Kuwaiti oil fields set on fire. On the twenty-fifth, radio communications report Iraq is now dumping oil into the Persian Gulf.

The night of 30 January starts like any other. I'm standing outside my tent, listening to my guys inside, horsing around. I look up at a sky beginning to fill with clouds but still open enough to catch the sight of aircraft passing high above, heading for Iraq. This has been routine, both day and night. Inside the tent, I go over tomorrow's schedule. Sergeant Brown comes in and calmly announces, "Everyone on the wall. Take everything with you, Staff Sergeant. This is not a drill. You are needed at the company CO's tent. ASAP."

I gaze at my watch to check the time—2045. "Copy that, Sergeant." To the men, I say, "Get your seven-eighty-two gear on and report to the wall. Sergeant Ford, make it happen."

"Aye, aye, Staff."

Putting on my gear with ammo pouches, canteen, and Ka-Bar attached, I pick up my .45-caliber pistol, insert the magazine, and chamber a round.

At the major's tent, the CO starts, "Several hours ago, an Iraqi force crossed the border with a mechanized division and an elite Iraqi brigade. They're in the town of Khafji, Saudi Arabia. Both Marine and Saudi troops are repelling that attack as we speak. However, another Iraqi armored brigade crossed the border earlier tonight. They're heading in our direction. Their last reported location had them within five miles of this command and closing. That was when we lost sight of them. At the moment, we have no idea where they are. Inform your Marines of what to expect. Any questions?" There are none.

I walk outside to what is now a cloud-filled sky blocking out any moonlight. The camp is set in total darkness. At the wall assigned to Motor T, I find the troops, including the Women Marines, standing on sandbags and peering over the wall. "Staff Sergeant, there's something out there," a Marine hollers. Stepping up to the one who spoke out, I look downrange and spot what is making him nervous. There, driving across our south wall, is a line of armored vehicles about a mile away. They're heading west and moving fast.

I say loud enough for all to hear, "Those are friendlies."

"How do you know, Staff Sergeant?"

"If they weren't friendly, you wouldn't see their blackout lights, and they'd be heading straight for us, not across our flank. Besides, if the Iraqis show up, it won't be at this wall, it'll be at the north wall." I point in that direction while stepping down. "If we get hit, and if you hear me yell to grab your trucks and go, you do it. These M-16s are not going to stop armor. Head south. You'll eventually run into friendly units."

These orders trouble me, but I know what the outcome of such a battle will be. Staff Sergeant Woods asks, "You telling us to run?"

"Woody, I was talking to a Marine from that unit to our front yesterday at chow. He told me they have four TOWS on two Hummers. Anything larger than a platoon of armor and they're toast, and so are we."

Woody looks concerned as I continue. "Keep this to yourself, but those Marines out there will not hold back a brigade of armor along with the infantry attached to that size unit. If they break through the wall, falling back and maybe saving some equipment is our best chance to fight another day. We're not going to stop that many Iraqis and those tanks with M-16s and only a hundred twenty rounds per man. We have no grenades, no anti-tank weapons, and a .50-caliber we don't even know works. What a joke. We'll be massacred." I let that sink in, and I can tell Woody agrees with me.

Through the night, I try to keep the Marines calm, but I can see they're getting edgy. When the gas attack siren goes off, we have to don our suits, and I get the feeling the battle is close. At the sound of helicopters closing in on our position, I look to the sky. Memories of battles past disturb my thoughts. I won't let that affect me.

The sounds of whirling blades grow louder and louder until, only feet above us, two Cobra gunships fly overhead, heading north toward the Iraqi tanks. It's about to start.

CHAPTER 22

MOVING OUT

A**S THE BIRDS FLY PAST,** I look up and see rockets attached to their small wings. The sleek choppers are on target for the approaching Iraqi tanks. From behind me, I hear, "Those Marines?"

I turn. It's the same Marine driver I met buying pogey bait in the truck stop on our first convoy to Al Jabar. Her lips and chin tremble as she looks at me.

"You know it, Lance Corporal." Walking to her, I ask, "Did you see those rockets, under their wings?"

"Yes, Staff Sergeant." I look around and can tell she's not the only one anxious about what's coming. All the Marines on the wall are. What I say next is for the benefit of all of them.

"Each one of those rockets can take out an enemy tank. Those birds are going to destroy that Iraqi brigade. You believe me, don't you, Lance Corporal?"

"Yes."

I smile, and she seems to relax and smiles back. "Good. Now keep your eyes out there, over the wall."

Pulling me aside, Woody says, "You know, those rockets were anti-personnel, not anti-tank."

"Yeah, well"—I look back at the wall—"they don't know that."

The choppers move out of sight, and quiet returns to Mishab. Hours pass, and we've heard nothing on the approaching tanks. I look at my watch, and it's 0330. Suddenly, two people coming from headquarters start yelling something garbled. A cold shiver covers my body. I fear the Iraqi tanks are here. Then the announcement they're yelling becomes clear. "Stand down. Stand down."

As my Marines step down from the wall, one asks, "Is that it, Staff Sergeant? We're not going to die tonight?"

I glance at him and then the lance corporal I talked with earlier. "That's right. It's over."

She looks at me and smiles.

Top arrives and tells Woody and me, "The CO wants every man back in his tent."

Before I leave, I order Sergeant Ford, "Get everyone turned in. Tomorrow is another day."

"Copy that, Staff Sergeant."

While I'm walking to the major's tent, Woody comes up on my left. "What do you think happened? I never heard any explosions or anything to our front after those Cobras passed by."

"I don't know. Hopefully we're going to find out."

We arrive at the command tent and walk in. The officers and staff are all talking to one another. When the major's ready, the first sergeant yells, "Attention!"

The major moves forward. "At ease. I have not had any direct confirmation on last night's enemy brigade, but I will tell you what I know." He moves to a map of Kuwait and Saudi Arabia that has replaced the lists of names on the pin board. "This is where the Iraq Brigade crossed over. After a mile or so, they turned right, and that set them on a heading, straight for us."

Pointing an inch before Mishab on the map, he adds, "This was their last known position."

The officers standing closest to the map mumble, and I slip my way in to get a better look. My platoon commander, Captain Morrison, says, "That looks closer than five miles, sir."

"That's correct, Captain. We dodged a bullet. Division HQ picked up the Iraqi tanks here." The major points at the map. "They were in visual range of our northern wall when they stopped their advance and returned to Iraq."

"They turned around?" someone from the back shouts.

"Yes." The major waits a few moments and then gives his

theory. "It's my opinion the Iraqis got close enough to see us. They saw the Marines out front. Behind those Marines was a unit they knew nothing about. Because of our unit size, they turned tail and headed home. Don't forget, we're the closest unit to the Iraqi forces. They must have figured we were a combat unit and not a support unit."

Major Zana, the XO, is a big man. He stands six five with a muscular frame that presses outward against his camouflaged blouse. "If they had not turned back, we'd be in a world of shit."

It could have been a French Dien Bien Phu. Wiped us out.

The meeting ends, and I return to my tent for some needed rack time. I lie down, but before falling asleep, I go over the night's events. The Iraqis have shown they're not afraid to cross the border and bring the battle to us. What will Command do now?

4 February 1991

I wake this morning ready to begin another day. I walk across the lot to the Motor T office, where Captain Morrison and Top are drinking coffee. "Good morning, sir, Top."

"Good morning, Green," the captain answers.

While I pour a cup of coffee, the captain gives me my itinerary. "If you haven't noticed, there are three trucks sitting in the yard, loaded and ready for you to take west."

Surprised, I respond, "I'm not taking them back to Jabar?"

"No, Staff Sergeant, you're not." The captain pulls out a map and places it on the master sergeant's desk. I step closer and try to follow what he's explaining. "We are here." He points at the map. "Here is where you need to go. I was there yesterday and marked it with a stake in the ground and a red flag. You can't miss it. You'll need to leave ASAP."

"That looks like a long drive, sir. What am I hauling?"

"The drive is long. It took me more than two hours in a Hummer yesterday. One truck has your tent, MREs, racks, and water, plus some miscellaneous gear. Another is ammunition. The other two have incidental equipment needed after the platoon arrives. The only thing you need to off-load is the truck with the gear for your stay. Pick your drivers and move out. I need you out there. Any questions?"

I have a million but need to ask only one. "How long will we be out there alone, sir?"

"I'm not sure. We've been told the whole battalion may be moving, but we're not sure when. If it happens, then we need a marker to come to, and that marker is you. So it could be a day, or it could be a week. Stay alert out there. As soon as you find the red flag, radio me." He reaches behind Top's desk and pulls out a PRC 77 field radio, almost identical to the radio of the Vietnam era, PRC 25. "This is your comm. There'll be someone here to monitor the radio twenty-four hours a day, in case you get into trouble."

I'm handed a sheet of paper with my orders, radio frequencies, and call signs.

"You are Mike Papa. We are Echo One Alpha. That's it. You have any more questions, ask them now."

I look at the map, and there are no roads where we're going. A desert map is not something I've ever used, so I ask, "Do you have a compass, sir?"

The captain pulls out his own compass and hands it to me. "Take care of this, Green. I want it back. In working order."

"Copy that, sir."

"Anything else?" he asks.

"Does this place have a name?"

"The only name I could find was 'gravel pit.' I heard from the battalion CO that General Krulak was naming the place Al Kanjar."

I know whatever is going on is high above my pay grade, so I answer, "No, sir, nothing else."

"Then move out."

"Copy that, sir."

As I move off to find my drivers, the captain adds, "Stay alert out there, Staff Sergeant. You're on your own."

With the morning formation over, the Marines head to the yard to do their vehicle preventive maintenance. I make a quick trip to the head and then go over to my tent to get my gear together. My plan is to pick my drivers from those in the yard.

I walk into my tent and find Sergeant Ford and a few Marines lying on their racks. They act nervous when they see me, and I'm thinking they're trying to escape the boredom of another day in the Motor T yard. I count their number aloud so they can hear me and say, "Seven of you. Sergeant Ford, I want you and these men, in formation, in front of this tent, now."

Back outside, I wait for the men to follow. They're not moving very fast, and I begin to wonder if I'm making a mistake taking these Marines. I tell them, "There are three loaded six-by trucks in the yard. The eight of us will be taking them west to find a new location for this platoon and the battalion."

Sergeant Ford is my top sergeant, and my friend. I'm surprised and disappointed I found him with these Marines. I make a mental note to speak with him about this later. I can't afford to have my lead sergeant start down the wrong path, so close to the beginning of the ground war.

I continue with the orders. "You will need to take all your personal gear, and I mean everything. We will not be returning to this base. You have fifteen minutes to gather it all up and be back here. That is all. Dismissed."

One Marine, Corporal Morris, wants to know more. "Staff Sergeant, what's going on? Why are we not coming back?"

I refuse to answer him or any questions about the mission. I don't have enough information, anyway, and staying quiet will do two things. First, it keeps me from giving out any info that may be wrong. Second, it shows them I'm not interested in sharing. They only need to follow orders.

Within thirty minutes, the men are back, and we're boarding the trucks. I tell Sergeant Ford he's driving the truck loaded with ammo. The beads of sweat on his forehead tell me this scares him. Arguing, he says, "I don't have an ammo hauler on my license. I can't drive that vehicle."

"Sergeant, we're in a state of combat. I don't care if your

license has ammo on it or not. You're my top driver, and you will drive that vehicle."

Reluctantly, Sergeant Ford climbs into the driver's seat. The convoy heads out, my map in the hands of my A driver, PFC McCally. He's a short muscular Marine who can't stop smiling.

"You know how to read that map, PFC?"

"I think so, Staff Sergeant. It looks pretty simple, as long as we keep going west."

I hand him the compass the captain loaned me, and we begin. We start out by following tracks in the sand that I'm hoping belong to the captain. After a mile or so, the tracks disappear, and I stop the convoy to get my bearings. I check the map and try to figure out where we are. The trouble is there are no identifying markings in the desert. For miles around, everything looks the same.

I spy a mound of sand blown into a beautifully shaped half-moon, like the crest of a wave frozen in time. The sand on it shines so brightly, it appears to be smooth to the touch. I'm tempted to drive over and touch it. See if it feels the way it looks.

I stare, and the sight has me remembering a lake from my boyhood. The sand around the half-moon has ripples, like the small lake where I fished. When the wind picked up on the lake, it produced waves rippling on each other, some only inches apart.

The sand I'm seeing has waves trapped without motion, all the rippling brought to a stop. Only this lake has a reddish yellow-green to it. So beautiful. I could stay and watch it all day.

"Staff Sergeant," PFC McCally calls.

I don't respond but continue to daydream.

"Staff Sergeant!" he says again.

Without a word, I put the Hummer in gear and move out in search of the red flag. The ride is long and bumpy, and the view is of endless sand. After several more miles, PFC McCally informs me, "We're close." I slow the vehicle to a crawl.

My A driver startles me when he shouts, "What's that?"

I turn in the direction he's looking. "Where?"

"There. Right there. See it?"

I strain to see, but there's nothing.

148

"Over there. About fifty yards." He points. "That way."

In the sand, I see what may be something red. I'm still unable to confirm whether it's what we're looking for. After stopping the Hummer, I hop out, and the A driver follows. The young PFC runs to the sighting while I trail him. I stop dead in my tracks when he bends over and picks up a stick with a red flag attached.

McCally runs back to me with his normal smile enlarged from ear to ear. "It must have fallen over during the night, Staff Sergeant. Woo-hoo," he yells. "We found it."

I smile as the other Marines are now out of their trucks and standing around. Finding the flag is a big deal because now I know we're at the right spot to set up camp.

We park the trucks and my Hummer in a formation that keeps them spaced apart. Getting the Marines organized and our shelter up for the night is my first job. "Sergeant Ford, get the tent out and assemble it. PFCs Callister and Quarie, get the chow out and stack it. Everyone take your weapons with you, locked and loaded. Be sure they're never more than an arm's length away from this point on. I have no idea what's in front of us. I only need to know they're not friendly."

The captain had a whip antenna affixed to my Hummer. This will give the radio a few extra miles to communicate. I unhook the antenna from the front bumper, allowing it to unfold into its upward position. With communications established and the tent up, I put together a fire watch for the night. I decide on a one-man, two-hour post. It starts at 2000 and ends at 0600. Neither Sergeant Ford nor I will stand guard.

Before it gets dark, I order two fighting holes to be dug in front of our tent, facing north. Lance Corporal Abendana, a Jewish Marine who tells everyone he was born in Israel, is digging the holes. He says, "Hey, Staff Sergeant, this desert is like cement. We can't dig any holes."

I walk over and look at what they've done so far, which is little. I grab the trenching tool from Abendana and begin to shovel. When the blade hits the sand, it stops cold, and all I hear is a clunk. Abendana is correct. The sand is like cement.

Our work complete, nightfall overtakes us. Even with a bright moon above, darkness settles in on the desert. We're in the middle of nowhere, and the eeriness of this vast space at night is like nothing I've ever experienced. All around, the blackness hides the desert, but the sky fills with a million twinkling stars. The sight of three dots flying in formation miles above tells me they're bombers, heading for Iraq. I'm reminded that, as in Vietnam, we own the sky.

Everyone has turned in for the night except for the watch and me. The day has taken a toll on these Marines.

"Keep awake, Marine. We don't know who's out there."

He nods.

I follow with, "Good night, Lance Corporal."

"Good night, Staff Sergeant."

I walk into the tent and lie down on my rack. I have no idea what tomorrow will bring, but I close my eyes, knowing whatever it is, we'll do the job.

A tremendous boom from outside shakes the tent and wakes us all.

"Grab your weapons and get outside," I yell.

"What the hell, Staff Sergeant?" a Marine yells.

What I see sends chills down my spine. I say, "I never expected that."

CHAPTER 23

THE WAIT IS OVER

A HUNDRED YARDS TO OUR WEST, the booming of outgoing artillery lights up the darkened desert. Everyone watches as bright-red blazes ignite like balls of fire.

Behind me, a Marine asks, "What's going on, Staff Sergeant?"

"That's SPG artillery. They're firing on the Iraqis. They must have moved in after dark."

"What's SPG, Staff?" the lance corporal who first saw the big-gun fire asks.

"SPG, Self-Propelled Gun. They look like tanks, but they fire the one seventy-five Howitzers. The big guns."

Just as quickly as they began, the blasts stop, and darkness returns.

"Wasn't very many. Why did they stop?"

"Most likely they're moving off. Listen. You hear the hydraulics? That's their stabilizers. They're bringing them up so they can book before the Iraqis fire back."

"So they fire, and then before the Iraqis can locate them, they're gone?" Ford asks.

"Yeah," I answer. "On to another area so they can do it again." With a grin, I add, "That has to drive the towel heads mad."

Minutes after the artillery stopped, explosions erupt where the gun was. Fire and sand fly high in the air.

"What the hell is going on?" a Marine behind me asks.

My eyes stay glued on the incoming. "The Iraqis are firing back. That's why those Marines booked." Then I add, "That Iraqi artillery is as good as dead. Our air will make short work of them."

But my real concern is that the Iraqis are within artillery range of us. If they see us, will they fire? "Let it go," I whisper. There's not a damn thing I can do about it.

The night passes, and in the morning, I get word the company won't be arriving for at least another twenty-four hours.

I assemble the troops and tell them what I know. "I've talked with Captain Morrison. We won't be reinforced today. I want a rifle inspection at ten hundred today. We need to make sure we're ready for whatever might come our way. If you need to clean your weapon, then clean it. Conditions out here can turn that rifle into a club." Later that morning, I finish the weapons inspection with positive results.

During the day, we witness a sight most have only heard about, the aerial refueling of fighter jets. The jets hook up to this long pipe coming out the ass end of huge planes. This is quite a sight. The sky is filled with our aircraft all day long. Fighter jets flying cover, bombers heading for Iraq, helicopters, gunships, and OV-10s. The firepower from above makes us feel safe. Even when we look around at how few we are, I know they are here with us.

Then, just after lunch, PFC McCally spots something interesting. Pointing at the sky, he shouts, "Hey, Staff Sergeant, check them out."

I look up and see three OV-10 Warthog tank killers. They're flying out of the south and passing a few hundred feet above us. Heading toward Kuwait, they're soon out of sight, and we hear rocket fire and then explosions. The men pump their fists in the air, yelling, "Ooh Rah!" I smile and realize after last night's artillery show, and the firepower those tank killers let loose, we're hitting their forward positions. That means the invasion is soon.

PFC Pulver is sitting in my Hummer on radio watch when he calls out, "Hey, Staff Sergeant, the captain is on the radio. Wants to talk to you."

I walk to the Hummer and pick up the handset. "This is Mike Papa. Go ahead, over."

Captain Morrison has a warning. "Marine units are reporting Iraqi desertions up and down the line. Some of Saddam Hussein's troops are just walking south and surrendering. Be aware, if they spot you, you might get a few. If you do, secure them and report immediately. Understood? Over."

"Roger that. Out."

I pass the information on, adding, "If you're on guard tonight and you see someone coming toward you, do not fire. Wake me. I don't want to kill any Iraqi soldiers who want to quit."

It's two o'clock when the Marine on guard wakes me. "Staff Sergeant, there's something out there, in front of us."

I throw my blanket off and walk outside in my bare feet. "Where?" I ask.

The young Marine is nervous as he points to the northeast, the direction an Iraqi would come from. "There. You see it, Staff?"

"I do. Whatever it is, it's not infantry. Too big. Damn, what I wouldn't give for a flare right now."

"It's moving again, coming right for us," he says anxiously. "You want me to wake the guys?"

I start to give him the okay then raise my hand and stop him. "You know what that is, Lance Corporal?" I look into his scared eyes. "It's a camel."

The Marine slowly looks across the darkness and watches a camel casually stroll past. He smiles. "No Iraqi prisoners tonight, huh?"

I say, "Nope, not tonight. I'm going back to bed. Stay awake." As I enter the tent, I add, "You never know."

The night passes with no Iraqis walking in on our position. In the early morning, Staff Sergeant Matters arrives with a few trucks and, behind her, the company. Battalion begins to filter in throughout the day. When the dozers start arriving, the berm wall around us goes up. By the following day, the battalion is in place. Motor T is together again, and the captain's in charge.

Two days later, Water Platoon has the showers up and running, and this time the water is heated. The one thing different about this base from the last is that the tents are all above ground. The sand is too hard to dig holes. That's good, especially after what happened in Mishab. We got saturated by a torrential downpour of rain, something I didn't think happened in the desert. The deluge was so great, the rainwater ran into the tents, filling them while we slept. When we woke in the morning, the water had risen to the top of our racks. I remember thinking, *I must still be asleep* as I watched my gas mask float by. I smile, until I remember the mess we had to clean up. I'm thankful that this time, we're above ground.

21 February 1991

The company falls in by the southern wall at 2100. I ensure that each member of my platoon has a canteen of water. This is our order. No one knows what's going on, but with the ground war near, I figure this could be the word we've been waiting for.

Colonel Marks, the battalion CO, begins, "Ooh Rah, Marines. I know you're all anxious to get this war going. I'm here to tell you, I am too."

While he pauses, I think, *This is it.*

"You may be thinking we know when this is going to happen." Looking across the company of Marines anticipating the news that we're going to war, he says, "I do not. We've been pounding the Iraqi line twenty-four hours a day, and it won't be long before we start kicking some ass." After more cheering, he says, "I have authorized the distribution of a new drug that will help you survive a chemical attack, if it happens. This drug is safe for you to take, and it will greatly diminish any nerve gas you're exposed to. It'll help you survive."

As the colonel continues talking, my mind returns to Vietnam and Agent Orange. I can't help remembering how the military said, "This chemical won't harm anyone." They got that wrong, and now they expect me to believe this is harmless bullshit.

My attention returns to the colonel as he finishes. "Platoon commanders, hand out the pills. Be sure every man gets one." After another short pause, he adds, "Take the pill, Marines. It can mean the difference in you living or dying."

The captain walks up and hands me the pills. "Make sure every Marine gets one, Staff Sergeant, including you."

"Copy that, sir."

With each pill sealed in plastic and in my hands, I face the platoon. As I'm handing out the pills, Corporal Baker asks, "You taking yours, Staff Sergeant?"

"That's what our orders are, Corporal."

"But are you taking yours?" Baker asks again.

"You have your orders."

My back to the platoon, I take my pill from its case. Then, after moving it to my mouth, I drop it to the ground in front of me. I quickly take a drink of water while stepping on the pill and smashing it into oblivion. I face the platoon, and some Marines are taking their pills while others have discarded them.

The captain walks forward with several atropine injectors. "If any of the Marines are missing an atropine shot, make sure they get one of these."

"Copy that, sir."

I tell the platoon, "I know some of you may have used your atropine for something other than a chemical attack."

PFC McCally laughs. "That rat ran around like crazy for ten minutes, Staff Sergeant, and then it, like, exploded. That was awesome."

I learned how Marines like the PFC went around and caught rats to inject them with their atropine to see what would happen. The drug speeds up the heart to counteract the nerve gas. The rats run around as if they're on fire until they die from an exploding heart.

"PFC, if you, or any of you, misuse this shot again, you might be signing your own death warrant."

"Understood, Staff. Won't happen."

23 February 1991

It's around 1900 hours. I finish a shower, and I'm drying off when Captain Morrison walks in. As he starts taking off his clothes, he notices me and moves closer.

"Glad I ran into you, Staff Sergeant. We go in the morning. Zero four hundred, our tanks cross the line, and battalion forward will be with them. You and your convoy right behind."

Suddenly my mind goes blank. I'm scared, no, terrified. I'm

like a convict on death row who knows the exact hour he'll take his final breath. I know, sometime over the next twenty-four hours, I, too, will take my last breath. The dream—a premonition, a warning, from all those years ago—fills my head. Every detail is suddenly fresh in my mind. I want to call Cindy and tell her goodbye, but I can't. *This is it. I'm going to die.* I want to run, to hide. Chills cover my entire body as I stand motionless. The captain continues talking, but I don't hear him, until he says, "Is there something wrong, Staff Sergeant? You look strange. Your face has turned white."

I snap back. "No, sir. Sorry, sir, just cold after my shower. You were saying?"

"Start lining up your trucks tonight. You'll have Dragons with ISO containers and four six-by trucks. You're loaded with everything battalion forward needs."

I get back in the game, clear my head, and focus on the mission. I'm a Marine, and if I'm going to die, what better way than in this uniform. "How many ISOs, sir?"

"Eleven. With your Hummer, you'll have a sixteen-vehicle convoy. I will have your next convoy ready when you return. We don't have thirty-two male Marine drivers to cover this, so you will utilize the female drivers as well. Any questions?"

"No, sir."

"We're going to lose people, Staff Sergeant. We could lose a lot of Marines tomorrow. If you get caught in one of those Iraqi ambushes..." He stalls, as if struggling for the right words, then says the only thing he can. "Good luck."

CHAPTER 24

IN HARM'S WAY

I ERASE ANY FURTHER THOUGHTS OF dying in the desert, convincing myself it's just a dream, and if it happens, so be it. I head to the tent housing Motor Transport office to find my top sergeant, Sergeant Ford. The MK14 flatbed Dragons are ready to go, as are the six-by-six trucks. We only need to place them in convoy order.

Inside the tent, I find the men are quiet tonight. None of the typical joking around and horseplay is going on. They don't know when the battle will begin, but they know the time is near.

I stare into the eyes of each man, wondering if he's afraid. I catch sight of PFC Tilly. His eighteen years seems too short to end here. Lance Corporal McCally's smile will soon fade. Corporal Baker is a tough Marine, bullheaded, but the kind I know I can depend on.

In Vietnam, the night before my first patrol, I was uncertain of the next day. I looked to those in charge as more than men giving orders. They were the men I needed to get me home alive. Now I'm the one with that responsibility. It's my job to get these Marines home ... alive.

"Sergeant Ford, I need to talk to you outside."

Ford's up and following me out of the tent. Smiling, he asks, "What's up, Staff?"

"We go in the morning."

His smile fades, and his shoulders tighten. His silence tells me he's afraid. I don't think less of him. Hell, I'm afraid. We should be. Neither of us can show this worry, not now. He knows the men need us confident when we tell them what to expect.

He relaxes and asks, "What are your orders, Staff Sergeant?"

"Walk with me."

I head over to our Motor T office. Master Sergeant Howard is sitting behind his green field desk studying a map. Looking up and grabbing some sheets of paper when we walk in, he says, "These are for you, Green?"

I take the papers. On them are the truck numbers and cargo that will be in this first convoy. "Yep, this is what I need, Top." I turn and walk out, and Ford follows.

"How many trucks going tomorrow, Staff?"

I motion him to follow. "Sixteen, including my Hummer. I want you as my A driver." Stopping in front of the tent hatchway, I tell him, "Get everyone over to the yard. We need to get the convoy ready."

I walk to the yard and look at eighteen Dragons lined up and loaded with ISO containers. Across from them sit six of the M939 series five-ton six-by-six trucks, also loaded and ready for battalion forward. I'll be taking fifteen of these vehicles on this first convoy. I'll need to sort them out tonight.

The men begin to file over and fall into formation. Before I begin, I wait for Staff Sergeant Matters. I know she's received word to be here with her WM drivers.

Matters arrives, and I begin. "In case you don't know already, the invasion will begin at zero four hundred tomorrow." I wait for some reaction, but none comes. The women seem relaxed. The news is expected, and they think they're ready. They're not.

"There will be sixteen drivers and sixteen A drivers going on this first convoy. I'm not yet sure who will be driving and who will assist. You'll find out in the morning. All the male Marines will be going, and some of the women as well."

Staff Matters behind me asks, "What about me? Did the captain or Top say if I was going?"

"Yeah, they did. You'll be staying behind to get the next convoy ready." Matters begins chewing her lip, clearly trying to hide her disappointment and frustration. "Why don't you talk with the captain and see if you can go as assistant convoy commander on the next run?"

She nods, and I begin to organize the convoy. I hand both Matters and Ford sheets of paper with vehicle numbers on them. "Staff Sergeant Matters, find these six-bys and bring them to the front of the yard. I want the four six-by-six trucks in front, directly behind my Hummer. Sergeant Ford, all the Dragons will follow."

The task takes ninety minutes, and when we're finished, I tell the platoon, "Everyone gets some sleep. You'll receive your truck assignment in the morning. Formation will go at zero three hundred. Whatever happens tomorrow, remember your training. If we get in an enemy arty attack, don't panic. Drive through it. You've been trained for this, and you're ready. PFC Tilly, what's the best way out of an ambush?"

"Pedal to the metal, Staff Sergeant."

I smile. "That's right, pedal to the metal. Tomorrow we kick some ass, Ooh Rah!"

Several Ooh Rah responses follow, then I dismiss the troops. Before they scatter, I tell Sergeants Brown and Ford along with Matters to meet me in the Motor T office at 2100. "We'll discuss troop assignments."

Back in my tent, I take out the list of names and begin assigning the driver and assistant drivers to each vehicle. I really don't know the WMs except for the two I met on that first convoy to Jabar. I assign them both.

I'm waiting inside the office when the three section leaders arrive. "Take a seat. These are the Marines and their truck assignments for tomorrow. Find the people in your respective details and make sure they know to be on the line by zero three hundred. I'm not sure when we'll cross. I guess that depends on how much resistance the Iraqis put up. I figure it'll probably be pre-dawn." I pause to be sure they're listening. "Sergeant Brown, you'll drive the last Dragon. I'll be leading the convoy, and Sergeant Ford will be my A driver. I've assigned the most experienced drivers. I fully expect to get hit with an Iraqi arty ambush sometime tomorrow.

Remember, if it happens, tell your people to push through. Make sure they understand, if a vehicle's hit, you push it out of the way and keep going. Check and make sure each Marine is ready. They'll need chow and plenty of water.

"Hold a rifle inspection tonight and make sure they take all their ammo. Every Marine will have their MOPP suit. Make sure they have their atropine and their seven-eighty-two gear is assembled and readied before morning." I hesitate, weighing my words. "Tomorrow is no joke. It's as real as it's ever going to get, for us all." Another pause. "See you in the morning."

They turn and walk out, and I stay and gather my thoughts. Tomorrow will not be the same war I fought in 1969. Tomorrow will be a war of high casualties in a short time. It will be bad for the Iraqis, and it could be bad for us.

February 24 1991

The duty walks in at 0230 to find me dressed and ready to go. "Oh, Staff Sergeant, you're awake."

"Yeah. Let's go."

We walk out into the cold desert darkness together.

"You get any sleep?" he asks.

"Enough."

I enter the Motor T tent. Top and the captain are both standing there sipping coffee. I acknowledge them. "Captain, Top."

The master sergeant nods, and the captain responds, "Get any sleep, Staff Sergeant?"

Seems like everyone wants to know how much damn sleep I got. "Enough, sir. Uh, sir, I want to get the convoy over to the berm wall as soon as possible."

"Copy that. As soon as you're ready, move out." I walk out of the tent then stop and turn back when I hear the captain say, "Good luck, Staff Sergeant Green. Bring 'em back home." I have no reply.

At 0330, the drivers are ready to go. The invasion is going to kick off in less than an hour. The men and women are quiet, but I can tell they stand ready. Should I say something? Try to encourage them, tell them we'll be okay? We won't. If we get hit with artillery, there's nothing to shoot back at. There's nothing we can do to make it stop. We can only run.

"Sergeant Ford, get the drivers into their vehicles. It's time to move out."

The drive to the berm wall takes about twenty minutes, but today it's taking longer. The whole Second FSSG is moving up to the berm. I look at my watch, and it's 0400. We continue to drive in bumper-to-bumper traffic, inching our way closer to our destination. Sergeant Ford has been quiet on the ride up but breaks his silence when he asks a question he obviously believes I can answer.

"Staff Sergeant, what's it going to be like?"

Before I can answer, a massive explosion to the north interrupts him. The sky turns blood red as fire burns high in it.

He yells out, "What the hell was that!"

I check my watch, and the time is 0430. The invasion has begun.

"That, Sergeant, was a Mine-Clearing Line Charge. One thousand seven hundred and fifty pounds of C-4 is exploding. Combat Engineers just blew a hole in the Iraqi minefield. Our guys are moving into Kuwait."

Another thirty minutes and the berm is finally in sight. The grunts have attacked, and the last of the M60 battle tanks are on their way. We hear *boom, boom* as the tanks keep firing.

The berm is different now. The wall that stood fifteen feet high is gone, because the bulldozers have leveled it. A master gunnery sergeant steps up to my window. "What's your unit, Staff Sergeant?"

"Eighth Engineers, Support Company."

He checks the paperwork in his hands and turns a few pages. "Here you are." He looks up at the trucks all lined up behind me and says, "You're a ways down the list, but I'll get you in as soon as I can." He points at a line of trucks. "Pull in behind that unit. If they move up, you move with them. Got it?"

"My battalion forward is already out there, with the grunts."

"They didn't go in from here. I would have sent them. If they're already on the move, they went in from a different launch point. Don't worry. When you get the word, you follow the road. It will lead you to them. Now get these trucks out of here. The whole damn FSSG needs to get in line."

The sun is rising on a day that will no doubt be filled with death. I wonder what God thinks about all this. Sergeant Ford gets in the Hummer. Joking, I ask, "Everything come out okay?"

With a smile I've not seen from him today, he answers, "As smooth as silk. I'm good for the whole day."

We both laugh.

The same master guns who's sent us here now has an unlit cigar hanging from his lips. He walks over to me. "What's your unit, Staff Sergeant?"

"Engineers Support Battalion, Master Guns."

"Okay, you're next. Move up to the line. Oh yeah, your unit forward, I hear they went in with two five." He's referring to the second battalion of the Fifth Marine Regiment.

"Copy that."

I start the Hummer and place it in gear while looking at Ford. "Here we go."

Even though the look on his face is serious, his voice cracks. "Let's do this."

The truck moves forward, and Sergeant Ford quickly reports the convoy is following. Up ahead is the hole in the berm where only a few hours earlier, Marine Corps infantry and armor launched the largest invasion by America since World War II. My Hummer moves through the berm wall and into the Iraqi minefield. The road is barely eight feet wide, and undetonated mines are only inches from our tires. A slip-up here can put a vehicle into those mines. What's worse is that many of them are chemical.

As we drive down this road, we follow a massive number of trucks. Up ahead, less than fifty yards away, are burned-out Iraqi tanks. Most have only their turrets sticking out of the ground. It seems the Iraqis dug holes and placed their tanks inside to protect them from our air assaults. This may have helped them survive death from above, but it took away their mobility, making them nothing more than pillboxes.

As we move deeper into what is surely Kuwait now, the road rises, leaving me blind to what is happening ahead. Suddenly, everything comes to a stop. We're sitting still with nowhere to go. Forward is blocked, backward is blocked. We can't go left or right for fear of the minefields. My worst nightmare becomes a reality.

The minefield erupts with an explosion forty yards to my right. Sergeant Ford says, "What the fuck was that!"

I don't answer because I believe it was enemy artillery. Another explosion to my left confirms my fears. Without thinking, I blurt out, "They've got us bracketed, Ford. The next rounds are going to be dead-on!"

His lips tremble as he cries out, "What the hell are you talking about?"

I try to remain calm even though I know this might be the end. "We're bracketed. As soon as those guns get confirmation, they'll rain down on us. Remember the Iraqi ambush the captain warned us about? We're in it."

"We gotta get out of here! Do something!"

"Do what, Ford? We're trapped."

He looks left and right then behind, and I see his fears take root. I try to calm the sergeant, telling him, "There's nowhere to go. Cool down. We'll be okay."

Ford pays no attention. He's scared. I get that. But when he shouts that he's getting out, I yell, "Stay where you are, Sergeant! That's an order!" I take a deep breath and say, "Think what you're doing. You want to tell those drivers Iraqi artillery is about to come down on them? Tell them they have two minutes to get their MOPP suits on? To get out of their trucks? What's going to happen?"

Ford stops, looks at the convoy, and says, "Not good."

"Yeah, man, not good." I give it a moment. "We order them to start evacuating their vehicles, they might panic. Guys might end up in those minefields. And where should I send them? Forward?

To the rear? What if they're caught in the open? Where will those shells land? It's best to stay in our trucks and ride it out."

Ford seems to accept our situation as he calms down and stares out the front window. "How many vehicles you figure are out here, Staff Sergeant?"

"Don't know. Could be a thousand."

"Out of all those trucks, why is our convoy the one bracketed?"

Without thinking, I answer, "It's because of me." Ford faces me and stares.

I sit back and wait to hear the shells come in. There's an old saying, "You never hear the one that's got your name on it."

CHAPTER 25

HADES

Still day one

THE FAMILIAR SOUND OF HELICOPTER blades echoes across the desert sand. "Here they come, Ford." The sergeant and I gaze upward as we watch two helicopters pass only yards above us, heading to the northeast.

Ford shouts, "Gunships!"

"Cobras, looking for that Iraqi artillery." I grin.

As the Cobras pass over, the Iraqi shells start to land. The first one hits twenty yards to our right, causing secondary explosions. The next hits to our front, barely missing a road grader tied to a lowboy trailer.

The choppers are no sooner out of sight than I hear a familiar sound, the buzzing of a billion angry bees. It's a sound I haven't heard in decades. "Those are mini guns, Ford."

The sound continues as the choppers fire on the Iraqi artillery. Then I hear swooshing sounds as the Cobras unleash their rockets. The explosions that follow tell me the enemy guns are destroyed.

This is not how I die ... today.

The trucks ahead begin to move, and we move with them. As we pass out of the minefield, Iraqi tanks and other armored vehicles are spread out across the desert. Most have been destroyed and are on fire.

Mixed in with the burning Iraqi tanks are other armored vehicles and trucks that seem to be abandoned. "What about those?" the sergeant asks. "Looks like the Iraqis left them there. What's that about?"

"I guess they ran away," I say.

Along our side, fifty yards away, sits what looks like an American tank. "See that one? Off to your right, Ford. That's a Marine Corps tank."

The tank sits still with its gun pointed downward. "Guess some Iraqis fought back. Think the jarheads made it out? Hope they did."

"I don't know." I stare at the destroyed American tank. "I don't see any damage. It's just sitting there. Maybe it stopped working."

Our drive continues, and many enemy vehicles, mostly trucks, are pointed north. I wonder, were they running away? Bodies of Iraqi soldiers begin to litter the ground, and their corpses stain the desert red with blood. "That's some gruesome shit, Staff Sergeant. I've never seen anything like this before."

"Pray you never see it again, Sergeant," I reply as my mind returns to the river filled with dead bodies that I witnessed twenty years ago.

As we continue, the desert around us is a junkyard. Destroyed enemy trucks are everywhere, and in them are the bodies of Iraqi soldiers. Some have been burned and mangled so badly, they're not recognizable as human. I'm right about one thing—this war has produced mass casualties, all Iraqi.

The convoy picks up speed, and after a few miles, we take a turn in the road and pass through another sand berm. There on my left, sitting on the ground, are several ISO containers and, among them, a trailer on wheels. Standing in the doorway of the trailer is the battalion executive officer, Major Zana.

A lieutenant hails me down. "You from Engineer Support Company?"

"Affirmative, LT."

Pointing at where Major Zana stands, he says, "That's headquarters. Line those ISOs up along the outer wall across from that trailer. Send those six-bys down the line. Company Supply's down there. They'll off-load you."

"Copy that." Explosions and small arms fire to the north have me asking, "The war sounds close, Lieutenant?"

"It is. We need that gear unloaded ASAP."

I get out of my Hummer, telling Ford to take the six-by-six trucks and find that supply unit and get them unloaded. While he goes off with those trucks, I get the Dragons lined up and ready to be off-loaded.

While I'm waiting, I spy a two-seater shitter. It sits alone in the open, uncovered.

There's nothing to conceal my activity, but I've got to go. I drop my trousers. I'm sitting there wishing I had something to read when I look up, and staring at me is the WM I talked with on the wall in Mishab. She's sitting in her Dragon, waiting to be unloaded. With my pants around my ankles, I start to pull them up but think what the hell. If she has to go, she'll have to do the same thing. I stay and finish what I started.

As I sit on the shitter, I check the time. It's noon, and the sun is shining bright in a clear sky. From the west, a deep black cloud approaches. Finished, I stand up to watch this eerie sight. The cloud moves until it's over us. In only minutes, the sun has disappeared. This darkness is like nothing I've ever experienced before. A black cloud has engulfed everything as far as I can see, and the darkness is so dense I can't see anything in front of me.

I stand in silence as an oily mist filters down, covering our vehicle's windshield and settling on our skin. I don't understand what's happening or where this came from. I ask myself, *What is it?* The sun was shining only moments ago, and now it's been wiped out of the sky. To the west, I see the cause. The filth is falling from above, and I wipe it off my face and peer into what I can only describe as Hades itself.

From a hundred to a thousand yards out, I see a land that now belongs to the devil. Pillars of fire are burning uninterrupted. They litter the countryside, hundreds of them. I stare in awe. The darkness, the mist of black silt all around us, is broken only by the fury of those fires. This is what hell must look like. Saddam Hussein has set the desert on fire.

Suddenly I'm brought back to the war by the company gunny. "Staff Sergeant Green, Major Zana wants to see you ASAP."

"Copy that, Gunny."

I gather my thoughts and walk to the command trailer. Inside are officers and high-ranking enlisted personnel. Their conversations are distorted as they talk over one another. I find the major in a back room, where a large table is covered with maps. He's speaking with another officer when I interrupt. "Major Zana?"

He looks up from the map he was conferring over and says, "You're Staff Sergeant Green?"

"Yes, sir, reporting as ordered."

"Grab some coffee, Green. I'll be with you in a moment."

I step back and leave the two officers while I go find the coffeepot. It's against the wall in a hallway between the major's back room and the large room I first entered. I squeeze my way to it and grab a cup when a small Marine standing about five five asks, "Can I pour you a cup, Staff Sergeant?"

Before I realize who I'm talking with, I answer, "Sure, thank you."

As we talk and I begin fixing my coffee, I notice the two stars on his collar. That's when I realize General Krulak has just poured me a cup of coffee. I'm in awe.

"So what are you doing here?"

Rubbing the back of my neck, I try to hide my nerves. "I brought up fifteen trucks for battalion forward, sir."

"How was the ride?"

"Good, sir. Had some Iraqi arty try to take us out, but a pair of Cobras took them down."

"You had plenty of air support on your way up?"

"Yes, sir. Made us feel real secure."

The general smiles.

A captain interrupts our conversation. "Staff Sergeant, the major's ready to see you now."

I look down at the general, asking his permission. "By your leave, sir."

"Carry on, Staff Sergeant."

I swallow the last of my coffee and follow the captain.

I move next to the major, and he turns my way, asking, "Can you find your way back to battalion?"

Confident, I answer, "Yes, sir, I can."

"Good. There are a lot of trucks scattered across this entire area. They're from units all across the FSSG. They need to get back to their units on the other side of the embarkation berm. They have no organization or any control guiding them. I need this area cleared, immediately. Can you organize and lead them back?"

"Yes, sir, not a problem."

"When you get back, tell Colonel Marks I need the following. First, communications. Get me more field radios and antennas. Two, water. We need water ASAP. And three, I don't want to see any more female Marines in my forward position. You got that, Staff Sergeant? Not another female."

"Yes, sir, no more women in the front lines. Got it, sir."

"Very well. Carry on."

I walk out, catching the eye of General Krulak as I leave the trailer. He smiles, and I nod.

Outside, I find Corporal Baker sitting in his unloaded truck, smoking a cigarette. "Can you lead us back, Corporal?"

"Roger that, Staff Sergeant."

"Good, you're leading the convoy. I want two sets of eyes on the trip back. I'll be right behind you. This convoy's going to be big. We're moving out and taking as many of these vehicles from FSSG as we can. Stay put until all our trucks are off-loaded and have fallen in behind you. I'll start lining up the others."

Afternoon passes, and evening arrives. The convoy is finally ready to move back to battalion. The black cloud still hangs over us, and fires continue to burn in the distance. I've gone from truck to truck, pulling in as many of the lone vehicles as I can find for the move back. Finally ready, I order Baker to move out, and as we do, I'm checking the size of the convoy. More trucks than I expected have fallen in line behind us. By the time we're back on the road, I'm leading more than a hundred vehicles.

Our trip goes better than I hoped for, until we reach the minefields. A sandstorm erupts, covering the entire area. With strong winds, the sand is blinding. It's impossible to see the whole convoy. I can only hope we stay together.

Though it's difficult, I follow Baker's taillights until we come to a crossroad that wasn't there on our drive up. Baker stops, and I exit to figure out which way we go. Walking to him is difficult as the wind and sand nearly knock me to the ground. Together we try to get it right before continuing.

"We came from the right, Corporal," I yell through the wind.

"Yeah, I agree, but why that new road to the left?"

"I have no idea, but we go right."

"Copy that, Staff."

Back in my vehicle, I follow Baker as he turns right. Then something ahead stops us cold.

A glance to Ford, and I shout, "What the hell!"

CHAPTER 26

BACK TO BATTALION

"WHAT THE HELL!" I SHOUT while straining to see through the blowing sand. Headlights are heading straight for Corporal Baker's truck. He hits the brakes, and I slam down on mine. Behind me, a hundred trucks do the same.

Pissed, I throw the door open. Outside the Hummer, the storm rages on. I've never been in anything like this in my life. Putting my hand in front of my face for protection does little to relieve the stinging sand.

Corporal Baker rolls his window down. "What's going on, Staff?"

Through the howling wind, I yell, "I have no idea. But I'm going to find out." Struggling toward the headlights of the vehicle that forced us to stop, I'm knocked to the ground by the storm. Reaching the driver's-side window, I question the PFC behind the wheel. "What's going on? I have a shitload of trucks lined up back there. I need to get down this road."

Someone sitting in the passenger seat answers, "You're going the wrong way, Marine."

Sticking my head in the vehicle, I shout, "This is the way we came out."

"It's not the way you go back. You should have turned left. Follow the road. You'll come to a prisoner staging area. From there you can find your unit."

I notice he's wearing captain bars. "Copy that, sir."

Thankful this didn't happen too far down the road, I tell Baker, "I'm going to turn around and lead the convoy back. You get yourself turned around and fall in at the rear. Don't get left behind. When I see you, I'll know I have everyone."

Baker nods.

In my Hummer, Ford asks, "What the hell is going on?"

"Engineers made a new road out. We're supposed to go left."

I do a three-point turn and drive to the next vehicle still on the main road before the split. After rolling my window down, I signal him what to do. He nods, and I'm off.

The storm seems to pick up as the convoy rolls again. The shrieking of the wind has become so loud it hurts my ears. The sand pounding into the Hummer sounds like a million BBs hitting all at once. Worst of all is the powder sifting through the doors and windows, covering both Ford and me.

Though visibility is next to nothing, I make out lights ahead. Finally we pass the berm wall we left through this morning. We're back. On my left are those lights I saw. They're all attached to tall poles and tied down to keep them from blowing away. Several hundred Iraqi prisoners huddle under the light, trying to survive.

I pull my truck over and form my convoy, allowing those who followed to pass by and return to their own units. I did my job. I got them back. When Baker's truck shows up, I'm ready to roll.

Our convoy enters through the gate at Battalion and travels to the Motor T yard, where we park. Even though the storm rages on, Top is out to greet us. "Battalion CO wants you to brief him as soon as you arrive, Green."

"Copy that, Top."

I tell Ford, "Refueling and post OPs can wait until the storm ends. Get the drivers' chow and then hit the rack. We'll be up early tomorrow."

"Copy that."

I drive my Hummer over to the Battalion CO's tent then stop in front of his hatchway. I step in and find him lying on his rack. Captain Morrison is here as well. He's sitting on a folding chair at a table in the middle of the tent, drinking what smells like coffee.

"Staff Sergeant Green, you're back. How did it go?" the colonel asks.

"Things went well, sir. I have a message from Major Zana." I report everything the major told me, including the part about no more Women Marines.

The colonel, almost chuckling, says, "That sounds like Zen." Small talk follows, then I'm dismissed.

"Did you have any trouble, Staff Sergeant? Were you on the road when the Iraqi artillery hit?"

Somehow he found out about the arty attack on the convoy. "Well, sir, none of our vehicles were hit, and no one was wounded. Cobras covering us took out the artillery before they could zero in. I guess it didn't seem like a big deal."

The captain stares as if he's about to tear me a new asshole. "Truck Company was on the same road, and we got a report they were hit with artillery fire. They lost one truck and damage to another."

"Any casualties?"

"Yes." He exhales a soft breath. "We don't know to what extent. When I first heard the report, I thought it might be you."

"No, sir. Like I said, some arty rounds landed close, but nothing happened."

"Very well. You have another convoy going out in the morning. Are you readying the trucks tonight?"

"No, sir. With this storm blowing, I figure we'll wait until it calms down. I'll get the men up around zero two hundred. We'll get ready then."

As the captain turns away, I ask, "Excuse me, sir, what about Staff Sergeant Matters? She wants to go as assistant convoy commander."

"I had planned to assign her, but after what Major Zana said, she'll have to remain behind with me. Get some sleep, Staff Sergeant."

"Aye, aye, sir."

Sometime during the night, the winds calm and the storm ends. The duty NCO enters my tent. "Staff Sergeant Green, it's zero two hundred. Time to wake up."

Snapping up, I answer, "I'm awake, Marine. You can go."

"Copy that, Staff Sergeant."

26 February 1991

I look at my watch and confirm it's 0430. Day two begins. It's been twenty-four hours since the battle began. Sergeants Ford and Brown have the men readying the convoy. We needed the extra time this morning, because our trucks are covered in sand. Cleaning them up and doing our pre-operation check takes over an hour. As soon as we're done, I tell my sergeants to line up the trucks.

The morning is cool and dry. I look up at a million stars covering the sky and wonder if I will ever see a sight like this again. The trucks are pulling out of the line and forming the convoy. Everything is going as planned.

I walk to the office and find Master Sergeant Howard sitting at his field desk.

"Morning, Green. Your convoy ready?"

"Not yet, but it will be. Where's the captain?" I ask while looking around the office.

"The captain is up at FSSG headquarters for an early meeting."

I pour some coffee into a cup I found in my tent. I confiscated it as contraband.

"Battalion forward began moving as soon as the storm was over, about two hours ago," Top says. "I guess the division is kicking ass, and they need to keep up. I have no way of knowing exactly how far they've moved. Make your way to their last known position and then find them."

"Copy that. Top, any report on what's going on up there?"

"Last I heard, battalion forward was hit with heavy guns after the storm ended. We got a report saying there was one wounded medevacked by chopper."

"There are Marines from Heavy Equipment Platoon with the forward unit."

"Anyone else?"

"Yeah, some electricians too."

Worried, I ask, "The man hit, was he from engineer support?"

"Not sure. I think I heard he was from Bravo Company, Third Combat Engineers."

Now I'm more worried. "I know the first sergeant from that unit. Did you catch the rank of the WIA?"

"No, I didn't. Get your convoy on the road, Staff Sergeant." Handing me my manifest, he adds, "Make it happen."

As the sun rises, we exit through the berm and head for Kuwait. The sandstorm has blown the road away. Large ruts left from earlier vehicles are all we have left to guide us. With the minefields still live, I follow the ruts.

Mile after mile, we drive the only road back to battalion forward. It's the same road as yesterday. When it becomes apparent we're the only vehicles on this road, I start to worry. Another mile and I'm relieved when we finally see another convoy ahead. We pull through the berm where the battalion was yesterday. Off in the west, the oil wells are still burning. Though the smell remains, the black cloud is now centered only over the wells. All of battalion forward is just empty ISO containers, so I keep the convoy moving north.

The road past the berm is flat, something I didn't expect. A few more miles and I see why. Two graders are leveling and widening the road. One is on the left side, the other on the right, and they're about twenty-five yards apart. I zigzag the convoy past them, waving as I go by. I recognize the drivers, who are from our company's heavy equipment platoon.

Traveling farther down the road, I begin to worry. I haven't seen any friendlies for almost a half hour. Through my side mirrors, I notice the graders have also disappeared. I remember the army truck that got lost before the war started. The news was, they ended up in an Iraqi prison camp in Baghdad. I begin to second-guess myself, thinking aloud, "This is the only road out here. We can't be lost. There's no way we drove past several hundred Marines."

Sergeant Brown answers, "No, we didn't pass anybody. This has got to be the right way."

Finally, in the distance, we spot another berm. As we near, I see Marines guarding a gateway. I pull through and let out a sigh of relief.

Another wall of sand sits twenty yards to the north. Everything is going that way as we push the Iraqis out. I pull the convoy parallel to the north berm. No sooner are we parked than a container handler pulls up to start unloading the ISOs. After two hours, the convoy is empty and ready to return.

Before we can get under way, a gunnery sergeant pulls up in a Hummer with a .50-caliber machine gun on top. He parks in front of me, gets out, and says, "I need your trucks to haul prisoners back to the rear."

"I have to get back. I have a lot more convoys to run."

"I'm telling you, Staff Sergeant, I need your trucks. There are too many prisoners to handle up here, and that makes for a security risk. Headquarters FSSG has ordered all trucks running empty to lend a hand. That's you."

With no desire to bump heads with this gunny, I agree. "Copy that. Where are they?"

"Follow me. They're on the other side of the berm, about a mile or so. You'll see the EPWs on the side of the road."

"Got it, Gunny. Uh, EPWs? I thought you said there were POWs."

"EPW, enemy prisoner of war. You didn't know that? POW is reserved for American captured prisoners. All your trucks have A drivers, right?"

"Affirmative. Why?"

"After you load the EPWs, you need to keep a weapon on them. Use your A drivers as guards. Have them cover those Iraqis."

I nod, and he's off as I follow, taking the convoy deeper into Kuwait. Though I have no map, I can tell by the sounds of tanks, artillery, and small arms fire ahead, we're very close to the battle.

A mile or two down the road, I see an amazing sight. "Holy shit," both Sergeant Brown and I blurt out. Ahead we see hundreds of Iraqi soldiers, all sitting down. A platoon of Marines is guarding them.

I stop the convoy along the road. The guards don't wait for the okay to start loading the prisoners, they just do. I watch as the Iraqis climb aboard my truck. The first man on sits in the middle of the flatbed, and as the others board, they sit around him until the truck is full. One of my drivers, clearly dumbfounded, asks, "What the hell are they doing, Staff Sergeant?"

"Exactly what they need to do," I answer.

"With no sides on our vehicles, how are they going to stay on while I drive down this bumpy road?" Baker asks.

"By doing exactly what they're doing. The first guy sits in the middle, and each man after him sits down. They work their way forward while holding on to each other and using the man in the middle as their anchor."

The driver gives me a glance, and I add, "Pass the word, PFC. All A drivers are to report to me ASAP." Within ten minutes, they're all present.

"You men will be riding in the back of these flatbeds, weapons loaded. These prisoners are still the enemy. If you're threatened, you'll shoot them. Any questions?"

One Marine from my reserve side of the house comes up and says, "I can't stand guard, Staff Sergeant."

"Why not, Peterson?"

He shows me his weapon, and I want to pound him to the ground. The rifle is so full of sand and rust, I'm unable to pull the bolt back. The weapon is better used as a club. "Get your driver over here, now!"

When the driver for the vehicle this man is attached to reports in, I ask to see his weapon. His rifle is serviceable and ready to fire. "I need a Marine with a working weapon guarding these prisoners. You have a problem with that?"

"No, Staff Sergeant."

"Good. He drives, you guard."

As the two men walk away, I call Peterson back. Chewing this Marine out will not be sufficient. I need to drive home the danger he has put us all in.

"You allowed your weapon to become unserviceable. Not only does that put yourself in danger, it puts every Marine out here in danger. If we get in the shit, what do you expect to do? I'm writing you up on charges as soon as we get back."

"But Staff Sergeant—"

Before he can say more, I interrupt. "You've broken a dozen articles in the UCMJ. You're in a world of shit, PFC. Dismissed." He turns and walks away.

As the Dragons are loading, I estimate there are four hundred Iraqi EPWs sitting in my trucks. Our convoy passes through the two berms of battalion forward and down the road now being smoothed by graders. I figure with no more setbacks, I'll be back in an hour, two at the most.

As the road cuts through the still-active minefields, there's another problem. Up ahead, two trucks sit next to each other, blocking the road. Not only is my convoy blocked but also every truck trying to get back for more supplies is stuck. There's no way to drive around, and the mines are dangerously close.

I've had enough, and putting my truck in gear, I yell, "Hang on, Sergeant Brown, we're going around!"

"You're crazy!"

I drive half off the road as I try to reach the stoppage. At times, my tires come very close to the mines. Sergeant Brown's face turns ashen white. I reach the blockage and yell, "What the hell is going on?"

"He ran out of gas, Staff Sergeant. I'm trying to give him enough to get back."

The one who has run empty has a load of Iraqi EPWs on his flatbed.

"Put that hose away and get your ass out of here. You can't block this road. You're holding up the war."

He follows orders and puts his hose away. Moments later, the road is open. I ask the other Marine, "What happened? Were you in a convoy?"

"Yeah, I was. They left me. Said I should wait for a wrecker. But I got all these towel heads."

"I'll let them know you're out here and get you some help. We can't hold up all these trucks just for you."

"Copy that."

Back on the road, we finally pass through the berm of the embarkation point. When a colonel flags me down, I stop the convoy. Behind him are enemy prisoners surrounded by concertina wire. This is the same place as last night, only now it has grown tenfold. There's at least a thousand Iraqis and a lot more Marines guarding them.

"This is where you leave them," the colonel tells me. "My men will start unloading one truck at a time. We need to count and search each one before any of them enter the secured area. Give me a couple of your men to help."

"Copy that, sir." Curious, I ask, "Sir, are you military police?"

"Affirmative. This is our job, but there ain't enough of us to handle this many prisoners."

"Copy that, sir."

I have Sergeant Brown and the guard from the lead vehicle report to the colonel. They're placed in a position to guard the Iraqis being off-loaded.

The colonel orders them, "If you hear that yelping sound they make, you start shooting. You got that, Marines? If they yelp or scream in a high-pitched voice, you shoot them dead."

CHAPTER 27

AN UNTHINKABLE SIGHT

SERGEANT BROWN LOOKS CONFUSED AT the order he just received.

"Brown, I heard the colonel. If you need to shoot, I'll back you."

Brown seems a little more at ease as he nods in response. I turn my attention to the lance corporal.

"You only fire if the sergeant does. Understood?"

He also nods.

I just keep thinking, *Please don't any of you scream.*

It takes a few hours before the enemy prisoners are off-loaded and secured. As soon as we're released by the colonel, I lead the convoy back to Battalion.

I walk into the Motor T office to report in. No one is there, not even an orderly. I'm tired. My guys are doing their post operations to make their trucks ready for in the morning, and I still have to do mine. I find a piece of paper on Top's desk and write a note. *Everything is good to go. No casualties, no damage to any trucks. Brought back over 400 enemy prisoners and dropped them at EPW camp. Finishing my post OP and hitting the rack.* I walk out.

In the yard, I find Sergeant Ford doing my Hummer's post operations. "Hey, Ford, thanks man. I'm tired."

"Figured as much, Greeny."

I stare at him and think how I haven't heard that name in a while. He looks worried. Using a nickname for your staff sergeant is not usually acceptable. But I smile and say, "Don't worry, man. It's been a while since anyone called me that."

He smiles back. "It's been a long time since we've been alone. You're my friend, Rick."

"Yes, I am. You almost done there?"

"Just have to check the oil. Go on. I'll finish up. See you in the mornin'."

A wave and I'm off to sleep.

27 February 1991

D-Day Three Begins

I'm awake, dressed, and outside at 0430. It's been seventy-two hours since the invasion kicked off. Sergeant Ford surprises me as he walks out of the duty hut. "No resupply convoy today, Staff Sergeant. Captain Morrison wants a formation, ASAP."

"Is he inside?"

"Affirmative. I'm going to get the platoon together."

"You're up early this morning, Ford."

He stops and says, "Yeah, well, Top saw me last night finishing your Hummer and said I had last watch as duty NCO."

I grin and walk into the tent. The captain and Master Sergeant Howard are sitting at his desk. "Staff Sergeant," Captain Morrison says. "Have the platoon assemble ASAP."

"Sergeant Ford is doing that now, sir. What's going on?"

"Things have changed. We won't be resupplying battalion today. Truck Company is assuming those duties. We have a different mission."

Sergeant Ford sticks his head in the tent. "Platoon is formed, sir."

Outside, the captain updates us on what that new mission will be. "Staff Sergeant Green will take as many trucks as we can muster north toward Kuwait City. All drivers will be utilized, the women too. You're going to pick up EPWs from an MP platoon two clicks north of Major Zana's last position. Staff Sergeant, you'll release the trucks to the MPs. Then, I want you back here."

"Sir, if we release our trucks, we won't see them or our drivers again. They could keep them for some time."

Clearly skeptical, the captain asks, "What makes you say that, Staff Sergeant?"

I walk closer to the captain so not everyone will hear.

"Yesterday, the gunny who used our trucks to move his prisoners wanted to keep them. I have a strong feeling if I'm not there, we lose our trucks."

Frowning as if he's still uncertain, the captain agrees. "Very well, you stay in command. Bring them back when the mission's complete. The last thing I want is for Forward to call for supplies and we can't deliver because our trucks are somewhere else."

"Copy that, sir." The platoon is dismissed, and the Marines report to the yard for assignments. The captain and Top walk toward the Motor T office, and I join them, asking, "Sir?"

"What is it, Staff Sergeant?"

"We had a problem yesterday. Well, more of an unusual order. I need clarification should that come up today."

The captain stops walking. "What order?"

"Last night, a colonel at the EPW camp wanted two of our guys to guard the prisoners being off-loaded. He gave an order I wasn't comfortable with. He told them, 'Shoot to kill,' sir."

The captain jerks his head back, as if shocked. "Are you sure that was the order?"

"Yes, sir. That was the order. He said, 'If they yelp or call out in a high-pitched voice, shoot them dead.' If we get that same order again, is it legal?"

The captain takes a moment then answers. "There is worry that the Republican Guard may surrender to infiltrate our lines. They could start an uprising within the prisoner camp. That yelping is some type of religious warning of infidels. The last thing we need is for such an incident to occur. We would have to pull troops from the front to counter an enemy in our rear."

"So if we're told to shoot them, we do?"

The captain tries to clarify the order. "If you feel an order is illegal, Staff Sergeant, then follow your gut. But understand this. If that scenario does occur, it could delay or even jeopardize our entire operation."

I return to the drivers to pass along the day's plan. While Matters, Ford, and Brown ready the trucks, I deal with Peterson. I figure if he has his weapon clean, I won't write him up. Such an action in a time of war holds severe penalties. Also, I share some responsibility. If I had ordered more rifle inspections, this would never have happened.

Peterson is walking toward the yard with his rifle in hand, and I call him over.

"Let me see your weapon, Lance Corporal."

He removes the magazine and pulls the bolt back, locking it for inspection. I take it from him and find the weapon clean. Handing it back, I'm glad I won't have to press charges. "You're free to go, Peterson. I'm not writing you up. However, this incident will show in your proficiency markings." After a hard stare into his eyes, I'm convinced he's learned a valuable lesson. "You're dismissed."

The convoy assembled, we're on our way. The sand road has turned solid from the constant grading, and I increase our speed to thirty miles per hour. It's not long before we enter Kuwait and soon pass through the berms from day one and two. Fifty miles later, we come to a crossroad guarded by military police.

"Where are you taking these trucks?"

"Wherever they're needed to move prisoners."

The same gunnery sergeant I dealt with yesterday is there, but he doesn't seem to remember me. "You need to go that way, Staff Sergeant." He points down the road to the northeast. "There are hundreds of Iraqi prisoners from the air strikes last night. We bombed the shit out of them. They're calling it the Highway of Death."

"Highway of Death? What happened?" I ask.

"Iraqis tried to run back to Iraq. Thousands of them fled Kuwait City in both military and civilian vehicles. Marine air wing and Navy jets wasted them good."

I'm intrigued. I step out of the Hummer and follow the gunny, trying to get more information. He faces me and describes what he saw.

"I drove up there early this morning. I've seen dead before but not like this. There were hundreds of vehicles, all kinds, and still burning. The sky was filled with fire and smoke. And bodies, they were everywhere, all Iraqi soldiers, all dead." This tough gunnery sergeant, who only yesterday had a cigar hanging from his mouth as he barked out orders, seems less boisterous today. "They burned to death, many still in their vehicles. I don't think I'll ever get that out of my head. Something like that changes you, you know?"

Pointing northeast, he continues. "Follow the road. It will take you west of Kuwait City. You'll see the EPWs and the Marines guarding them."

All I can say is, "Copy that."

Back in my Hummer, I lead the convoy northeast. I explain to Ford what the gunny told me, but neither of us can truly comprehend what lies ahead.

Time passes, and I begin to worry. I tell Ford, "Keep your eyes open. I don't know if there might be Iraqis out here still fighting."

Another hour and up ahead we see people sitting in the sand. "Hey, Staff Sergeant, there they are. Those look like Iraqis. And those are Marines walking around them."

"That's it. That's what we're looking for."

As we pull up, a sergeant comes to my vehicle, asking, "You here for prisoners?"

"Yes, I am."

"How many can you take?"

"I've got twelve flatbed Dragons and seven troop carriers. We should be able to handle as many as seven to eight hundred."

"We have more arriving all the time, but that will help. Pull your trucks up, and we'll start loading."

The MPs are handling the prisoners, so I'm not needed. I have an urge to seek this Highway of Death. I make my way to the front of the encampment, where a captain and two staff NCOs are talking. "Excuse me, sir. I heard about this road called the Highway of Death. Can you tell me where it is?"

A first sergeant standing with the captain answers, "About five miles down the road. Kuwait City will be on your right. Follow the first right-hand turn you come to. Don't miss the turn. You'll end up in Iraq. Follow it all the way to Highway 80. That's the Highway of Death."

"Thanks, First Sergeant. These trucks are going to take a few hours to load. I'm going to head over there and check it out."

The captain warns me, "It's not a tourist attraction, Staff Sergeant. Don't get in the way."

"Copy that, sir."

I locate Sergeant Ford talking with other drivers. "Ford, get in the Hummer. We're leaving."

"Where we going, Staff?"

"To find that Highway of Death."

Together, we head toward the Iraqi destruction. After an hour, we finally see the road and turn right, heading east. The sand softens, and soon we encounter larger and larger ruts. We travel across a few more miles when, several hundred yards ahead, I see the destruction the gunny talked about. I stop the Hummer.

"You see that, Staff Sergeant?" Ford sounds as if he's astonished.

We step out of the vehicle to get a better look. Even after knowing what the gunny explained, I'm not ready for what I see. The destruction our air brought down on those retreating Iraqis blows my mind.

"Do you think we can get closer?"

I answer, "We're sure as hell going to try."

As we near the destruction, the road disappears, and there's only sand. I drop the Hummer into low gear and keep my speed slow. As I get to within ten yards of the wreckage, I stop and exit. Ford and I walk the last thirty feet. I'm shaken by what I see. In all my time at war, I've never seen a sight like this. We continue to get as close as we can, and I damn myself for not having a camera. In the carnage, I can see more than one dead body lying on the ground. Others are burned and mangled beyond recognition, still trapped in their vehicles.

Someone shouts, "Halt!" Two Marines wearing military police armbands walk toward Ford and me.

"What happened here?" I ask.

"Who are you, and what are you doing here?" one Marine asks.

I need to have a story, so I make one up. "I have twenty trucks picking up EPWs. I needed to find where this place was."

They seem to be okay with that story, so I press them and ask again, "What happened here?"

Now relaxed, the guards aren't afraid to share what they know. "The whole damn Iraqi Army was trying to escape last night. Air wing tore them a new asshole."

"What about all the civilian vehicles?" Ford asks.

"The towel heads stole anything they could drive. I heard our captain telling some major there were all kinds of loot in those civilian cars."

"Loot? What kind of loot?" I ask.

"Shit, I don't know. I heard there were paintings, gold, jewels. A bunch of stuff."

Sucking in a quick breath, I reply, "Awesome, man. Awesome."

One thing I remember from my time in Vietnam is the smell of death. That same odor is here. "You smell that, Ford?"

"Yeah, I do. How do you two stand that smell?"

"Don't know. It smelled worse earlier," one of the guards answers. "Guess we're just getting used to it. Besides, most of them burned to death in their vehicles."

I look at the slaughter, the absolute and total destruction. Burned vehicles and charred corpses litter the landscape. The destruction extends as far as I can see. I can't grasp what I'm witnessing, not on this scale. "Come on, Ford. We gotta go."

Ford continues to stare until I shout, "Ford! Let's go." He follows me to the Hummer.

Our drive back is quiet. Neither Ford nor I have much to say after what we witnessed.

"You okay, Sergeant?" I ask.

Ford's eyes never leave the road. He doesn't answer. I give him a minute or two, and then in a louder voice, I ask again, "Ford. Hey, man, what are you thinking?"

"I don't know. I've never seen anything like that. I don't know how I feel." Turning to me, he says, "What am I supposed to do with that, Rick? How do I tell folks what I saw?"

I don't have the answer to help him. Shit, I don't know what I'm going to do with what I just witnessed myself. "Maybe we don't say anything. If asked, we just say … couldn't find it."

In a low voice, Ford agrees. "Yeah, you're right. We just say nothing there to see."

The drive continues in silence. When we arrive at the detention area, I find the convoy waiting. The captain I talked with earlier stops me and asks, "Did you find what you were looking for?"

"Yes, sir" is all I offer.

"This area is not secured, Staff Sergeant. You could run into Republican Guard." He turns to stare at the prisoners. "There could be Iraqis out there wanting revenge. Stay alert."

CHAPTER 28

DANGER LURKS

I HAVE NINETEEN VEHICLES TRANSPORTING OVER seven hundred enemy prisoners of war. With only one Marine guarding each truck of forty or more, I'm concerned. I can't help wondering what might happen if there are any Republican Guard mixed in with these EPWs. What if an uprising starts? Or they make a move on the guard? If a Marine overreacts and kills a prisoner, what then? So many things can go wrong. I look in my mirrors and see that for the time being, all is well. The prisoners seem to have accepted their fate, and I hope they're happy to be alive. With a hundred miles to go, anything can happen. Our forces went through this area so fast it wouldn't surprise me if an enemy unit was overlooked. This desert is massive.

The MP captain warned me of that possibility. We need to stay alert.

"Sergeant Ford, keep a lookout for anything out there that doesn't look like it belongs."

"What am I looking for?"

"There could be Iraqi units out here that have decided to fight rather than surrender. If they've been watching this road, they'll have put H and I artillery strikes on it."

"You mean an arty ambush?"

"Exactly, now watch for forward observers on the sand. Look for Vehicles without an inverted *V* or anything that looks out of the norm."

Nervous, Ford rubs his hands on his trousers. After he pulls his weapon up and points it out the window, he appears to concentrate on what's out there.

Time passes, and I long for those crossroads we went by on our way up. I know once I'm there, the chance of an artillery attack or an Iraqi ambush will lessen. Before we can reach that safe haven, my fears are realized. His tone more curious than alarmed, Ford asks, "Staff Sergeant, what's that?"

"What, Ford? What do you see?"

While pointing out the window at a forty-five-degree angle, he says, "There. On that berm. That pile of sand. You see that? Is that a man?"

I look in that direction, straining to see what he sees. Then I spot it, not one but two enemy soldiers lying down in the sand about twenty meters to our right. It appears one of them has binoculars and the other, a radio.

I yell out, "Fire on them, Ford! Shoot them bastards. Hurry." But it's too late. As Ford is firing his weapon, the first Iraqi shells begin to land. The explosions are to our left, a few meters off the convoy. I speed up, hoping my drivers know what to do.

Again I'm yelling, "They're overshooting!"

I use my mirrors to check the convoy. The drivers are doing exactly what they've been trained to do—drive through the ambush as fast as they can until they're out of the kill zone. All that training is paying off and saving their lives and those of the prisoners too.

"We gotta get out of this ambush. It won't take them long to adjust fire!"

Looking back at the convoy, Ford yells, "Truck three got hit!"

I watch my mirror as a cloud of sand and smoke covers the number three vehicle. It looks as though it got hit, but an instant later, it drives out of the smoke.

"He's okay. He made it," I yell out.

A few hundred meters more and my Hummer disappears behind the cover of another natural sand berm. I stop so Ford and I can exit. The first truck passes by, its prisoners holding onto each other so they won't fall out. He slows down, and I wave my arms, hollering, "Keep going! We'll catch up. Don't stop for anything!"

The convoy continues until the last truck has passed by. No more enemy rounds are coming in. The attack is over.

"How many arty shells landed?" I hurriedly ask.

"Not sure, Staff. Three, I think."

"Yeah, that's all, three. Shit. I need to take a look."

I climb the sand hill and look on the other side. Ford is next to me. Lying on our bellies, we search for the Iraqi spotters, but they're gone.

"What do you think, Sergeant? Where'd they go?"

"Not sure. Maybe I hit one of them."

Still searching the dunes, I answer, "Yeah, maybe. Maybe you did." I pause a few more seconds. "Let's go. We gotta catch the convoy."

Back in the Hummer, we haul ass. As we get caught up and begin to pass, I tell him, "Look over those vehicles as we go by. Let me know what the prisoners are doing and if you see any damage to the trucks."

"Why didn't they adjust fire? They had time, didn't they, Staff?"

"Yeah, they did. I don't know why. They could have done some real damage. Could be they didn't want to fire on their own people. Or your shot hit them or scared them away. We'll never know. Thank God that for whatever reason, it didn't happen."

Back in the lead, Ford reports, "I didn't see any damage to the trucks, and the prisoners are okay. You know Kawalski, Staff Sergeant?"

"Yeah, he's the guard on truck three."

Ford starts to laugh. "I think he shit his pants."

Grinning, I ask, "Why do you say that?"

"Because he had his hand and eyes down his trousers. He was looking at his ass."

Ford and I both laugh as I try to picture the sight.

Up ahead, the crossroad comes into view. As we approach, the MPs wave us through. Another hour and we arrive at the prisoner holding camp. It will soon be dark, and the MPs waste no time removing the prisoners from the trucks. I step out of my Hummer and watch the Iraqis shoved to the ground with their hands raised then forced to kneel. A master sergeant confirms the reason I stayed with the vehicles today. He tells me, "Have your drivers form up. You're needed for a trip back. There are more prisoners."

I stop him. "I'm sorry, Master Sergeant. I need to get these trucks to my battalion. We have an important mission scheduled."

"I've got priority over any mission, Staff Sergeant. That comes straight from FSSG. So you can stay with them or leave. It's up to you, but they belong to me."

What an asshole.

The drivers know my rule. When the lead truck rolls, they follow. When the last prisoners are off-loaded, the master sergeant walks away. I move to the lead vehicle and tell the driver, "Head over to the fuel farm. I'll meet you there. We're not going anywhere but back home."

He smiles, puts the truck in gear, and heads out. The convoy follows. In the confusion of prisoner count and security, the master sergeant doesn't notice we're leaving.

Nudging Ford, I tell him, "Get in the Hummer. You're driving."

I return to where the top left me. As soon as the last truck is on its way, I run to my vehicle. Hurrying inside, I yell, "Go, Ford, go!"

I hear the master sergeant yelling, "Where the hell did those trucks go?"

"Don't stop, Sergeant. Not for anything."

As we drive away, I hear him scream, "I told you, they belong to me!"

I wave and smile. The master sergeant glares back.

The fuel farm is east of Mishab, a good twenty miles from the detention center. It will take close to an hour to get there. The time we spend fueling these nineteen trucks and my Hummer is going to add even more hours to this day. We won't be back to the Motor T yard until midnight. If we have a run tomorrow, we won't have time to get ready for it.

Once at the Farm, we pull our vehicles up to huge black rubber bladders. Several of them are spread out over an area covering hundreds of square feet. A berm fifteen feet high surrounds the entire fuel farm. The bladders are ten feet high and filled with gas and diesel. The Marines working in this fuel yard are able to fill only two vehicles at a time. When the fueling is complete, it's 2100 hours, and darkness has descended. I take the trucks back to Engineer Support Company, heading west ten miles down a desert road. We find our way back to the Motor T yard where Captain Morrison is waiting.

"How did it go, Staff Sergeant?"

"It went well, sir. We picked up around seven hundred prisoners, caught some Iraqi artillery on the way back. Almost had our trucks stolen by this master sergeant. Other than that, a normal day at war, sir."

With a broad smile, he asks, "What about the arty attack?"

"Only three rounds, sir, then they stopped. Could have been real bad. I had my A driver open fire on two FOs we spotted on a sand hill. He might have hit one or scared them away. It's possible, after they saw we were hauling Iraqis, they stopped their attack. But I don't know, sir."

"Go into the duty hut and find the coordinates on the map of where you took those rounds. I'll need to report that to headquarters."

"Copy that."

"You said something about our trucks being commandeered? How did you keep that from happening?"

"I waited until he had his hands full with prisoners and sneaked away."

The captain grins. "I'm not sure what we're doing tomorrow. So far there are no requests, but if they come in, you'll take 'em out."

"Aye, aye, sir."

"Get those coordinates for me, then get some chow and sleep."

D-Day Four

Ninety-three hours since the invasion began. It's 0100 hours, and I'm awakened after only two hours of sleep. "Staff Sergeant, we have an emergency. I need you to get your drivers up and in formation, ASAP."

CHAPTER 29

GOOD TO GO

D-Day four

I T'S 0115 AS I WALK out of the tent to a cool and clear night. I take advantage of this cloudless sky to look up once again at a heaven filled with stars. It doesn't get old, staring into the night. This desert sky is endless.

I glance to the yard and see the captain reading something with the aid of a flashlight. Inside the tent, I hear the Marines stirring, and I know they're awake. I walk to the captain. "Good morning, sir."

No response.

Behind him, I watch Marines loading ISO containers and two six-by-six trucks. "What's going on, sir? What's the emergency?"

"Battalion forward is planning a move into Iraq. We need to find them and deliver these supplies ASAP. I'll be taking this convoy north myself, but I want you as my driver."

"Aye, aye, sir. Who's doing the loading?"

The captain turns in the direction of those Marines and begins to walk toward them. "They're Supply. I've already ordered an ISO loader."

He stops and hands me the flashlight along with his paperwork. "This is everything that's going. Supply has the same manifest. Make sure they get it all." He leaves me and walks toward the Motor T office.

Being relieved of convoy commander doesn't bother me in the least. The captain has probably wanted to get out of here and see what's going on for himself.

From behind, I hear the men walk out of their tent, and I turn to see exhausted Marines. Since they've had only a couple of hours' sleep, I can't blame them. Yesterday was one for the books. We drove two hundred miles over a bouncing road, endured an Iraqi artillery attack, then guarded all those prisoners. It took a toll on us all.

Once the platoon is in formation, the captain speaks. "Less than an hour ago, battalion forward was on the move again, heading into Iraq. The focus of ground combat action has shifted to northern Kuwait. We have Marines in southern Iraq."

Voices mutter over one another upon hearing this information.

"The division is shifting its main headquarters command control to that area. Our own battalion forward is in route now to support the move. Supply is loading the necessary ISO containers with everything requested by Major Zana. Gentlemen, we are seeing our Corps' success unfold right before our eyes. The supplies we deliver today will further advance victory. Staff Sergeant Green, assign driver teams."

I respond with gusto. "Aye, aye, sir."

My sergeants and I identify the vehicles and assign the drivers. The loading of ISO containers continues as the drivers perform their pre-operation inspections. At 0430, Sergeant Brown reports the convoy is good to go. The captain gives the order, and we move out, my Hummer in the lead.

"This is going to be a long ride, sir. Are we crossing the line while it's still dark?"

The captain stares ahead and seems preoccupied with something he's not sharing, "We cross now. I want to get these supplies there ASAP."

While on our way, we pass what used to be the berm wall separating Iraqi troops from ours. The hole I drove through four days ago is gone. In fact, the berm itself is almost all gone.

A short distance later, a sign on the side of the road reads, "Kuwait, 200 meters." We continue to follow until we come to a final crossing. Three Marines guard an opening protected with concertina wire. Two of them have rifles, and the other is wearing a sidearm.

The Marine with the sidearm holds up his hand to stop our convoy. As he crosses in front of the Hummer on his way to speak with the captain, I see he's a young lieutenant. "What are you carrying, Captain, and where are you going?"

"Resupply for Eighth Engineers Battalion Forward."

"I'm sorry, sir, but Command has ceased all operations forward. That includes all convoys until further notice."

"Eighth Engineers is moving into Iraq this morning, Lieutenant. These supplies are critical."

"I'm sorry, sir, nothing forward. You'll have to turn around."

Captain Morrison looks disappointed. For this entire war, Marines like him have been stuck in the rear with the gear, and now he wants to be a part of all this. The captain isn't moving, just staring out the window.

The lieutenant shows no patience. "I'm sorry, sir, but you need to return to your base, and you need to do it now."

The captain faces me and says, "Let's go, Staff Sergeant, back to Battalion."

I turn the Hummer around, and the trucks all follow. I can't help wondering what the captain is feeling. I think he knew this was about to happen, and that's why we're crossing before daylight.

"Is the war over, sir?" I ask.

"I don't know. Yeah, I think so."

It takes a couple of hours to get turned around. A lot of convoys are in situations similar to ours.

As we pull through the gate of Battalion, it's obvious word has spread that the war is over. We drive through the base, and there's almost a party atmosphere. Marines are all celebrating. Everyone we pass is laughing and cheering.

At the platoon area, the captain releases the drivers to their tents for rest. He orders a platoon formation for 1030 hours.

Back in formation, the troops are all anxious to learn how soon we'll be going home now that the war is over.

Captain Morrison passes the official word. "At zero eight zero one today, all hostilities were stopped. The war is over."

Marines cheer with Ooh Rahs.

"Saddam Hussein has capitulated, accepting all conditions of the United Nations."

Corporal Baker asks, "When we going home, sir?"

The captain has to smile and responds, "We have a lot of work to do here first, Corporal. Staff Sergeant Green, get the convoy unloaded."

"Aye, aye, sir."

Later in the day, Colonel Marks, the battalion CO, calls a meeting of all company heads. He repeats what we already know. "Saddam Hussein has accepted the terms of surrender. The president ordered all hostilities to halt at zero eight hundred hours. General Boomer ordered a halt to all further movements north four hours earlier."

I watch the colonel as he moves his gaze across the room from man to man before he continues, "We have a new mission now. I'll keep you informed on what your role will be as soon as possible. Until then, let your men celebrate. All weapons will be unloaded and kept that way until they're collected. That is all I have for now. Congratulations on a job well done."

"Ooh Rah" echoes out from everyone in the tent.

4 March 1991

Today I'm informed of two important activities. The first will be to collect all the weapons. Only those on guard duty will be armed. Second, we're to prepare to start hauling everything back from the north.

Master Sergeant Howard explains what he's learned. "Marines up north have gathered all the gear together so we can pick it up and convoy it back here. As soon as we complete that, the next step will be the wash line."

"Wash line?"

"Yeah, every vehicle, every piece of equipment returning stateside must be cleaned of all foreign substances before loading them for home. Get your convoys up and running. Use Staff Sergeant Matters as assistant convoy commander and the female drivers as well."

"Uh, Master Sergeant, can Staff Sergeant Matters take the convoys north?"

The top squints before he answers. "You getting tired of those trips, Green?"

"Yes, I sure as hell am." With a smile, I add, "I don't think my back has ever been this sore."

Howard chuckles and says, "You take the first one. Make sure she knows where she's going. If you're comfortable with her handling the missions, then make it happen. She'll enjoy that."

18 March 1991

Our reserves who were separated and sent across the battalion as needed when we first arrived came back today. All our officers, staff NCOs, and enlisted are together again. Twenty-four hours later, we receive the order to prepare our vehicles for the wash line. Going home can't be too far off now.

1 April 1991

"Hurry up and wait" is Marine Corps policy. Because of the massive number of vehicles, it takes until today before we're cleared to the washout. It feels strange, but I'm relieved knowing I'm on my last convoy in this part of the world. The equipment we're leaving behind includes the reverse osmosis for clean water. We're also leaving generators for power, the tents we stay in, and the aid station. The chow hall went down two days ago, so it's MREs until we leave. What we can't carry with us will for the time being be left for units designated to remain in Saudi Arabia.

With April comes the desert heat. When we arrive at the wash station, it's quite noticeable how many Women Marines are on the line. Like their male counterparts, they're attempting to beat the heat. All those on the line are in their green skivvy T-shirts. Those skivvies are getting wet and clinging to their bodies. I know my male Marines appreciate the show, but the Saudi government will not. It won't surprise me if they insist on the women covering up or being taken away.

22 April 1991

I'm sitting around this morning, just killing time, shooting the shit with Ford and Woody. One of my men walks over and tells us, "Did you hear the Saudis had all the WMs removed from the wash line?"

"Negative," I respond.

"Yeah, they said the women were being lewd and disrespectful."

"Looks like you had that right, Rick," Woody says.

"Yeah, I couldn't see how the Saudis refused to allow Bibles in and yet would allow our female Marines to be seen that way."

Ford smiles. "Too bad for us."

With most of the equipment gone, the company waits for final orders to return home. The troops are bored and restless. I hear about a television with a VHS player and a large number of movies in the officer's tent. This equipment should be for the troops. I head straight over, and walking into their tent, I argue for the troops to get the movies. I remind everyone that an officer can walk into the enlisted tent anytime they want to watch a movie, but the enlisted cannot walk into their tent. They were not happy but had to agree. I have a few Marines follow me back to their quarters and retrieve the equipment and movies. That night, the company shares some videos. No officers show up.

1 May 1991

The word is in. We're going home. Last night, the news we've all been waiting for finally arrived. Buses will be here in the morning to take us to where we all started from, Al Jubail airport.

I pack my personal gear. Carefully, I place in my bag the pictures Cindy sent me along with a camera, a Christmas doll, and my Walkman radio. She always made sure I had a new Walkman every few weeks since the desert sand destroyed them pretty fast.

It's Wednesday night. Funny I should think about the name of the day now. All this time, my only thoughts have been the dates written on my daily orders. Now, as I'm going home, I remember it's Wednesday.

"Hey, Greeny," Woody says as he walks into the tent. "You packed, man?"

"You better believe it. How 'bout you? Packed yet?"

"Nah. But I will be." Woody sits down on his rack. His eyes tell me he's unsure of something. He asks, "We did it, didn't we?"

I look over at him and smile. "Yeah, we did it, Woody. We won."

Morning arrives, and so do the buses. They're the same ones that brought us here months ago. We load up and are under way by 1000. Back at Al Jubail airport, a 747 sits on the edge of the runway. We line up single file and begin to board. On the plane, I sit in the business section, relaxing in one of the huge reclining seats. Woody is next to me, and his smile is genuine. As the plane takes off, Woody and I talk about what lies ahead. I learn that, like me, he can only think of what awaits us when we arrive in America.

I close my eyes, and my thoughts return to a telephone conversation I had with Cindy only a few days ago. I told her I'd have to spend some time at Camp Pendleton before they let us go. I explained how there'll be record books and pay to straighten out, and the Corps will want to do a final physical exam.

I remember her crying when I told her I'd see her in a week or two. She kept telling me how much she loved me and how the whole town would be celebrating my return. I still remember how America treated me when I returned from Vietnam. I remember the paper bags filled with shit thrown at us. And the red dye mimicking blood that was spilled on our uniforms and thrown in our faces. There'll be no name calling this time. This time, I and all those who served will be respected for what we did. This time I will be ... welcomed home.

CHAPTER 30

HOME

AFTER THREE WEEKS AT CAMP Pendleton, the Marines of Engineer Support Company want to go home. We've taken our physicals, gone through our record books, taken care of pay, and received all our awards. With our discharge from active duty in hand, we're returned to reserve status. Now the only thing left is the bus ride to the airport and the airplane home.

21 May 1991

The news finally arrives for the company. We're going home. The Marines are excited, so much so that no one is going to sleep. By 2200, everyone is packed and on the road. The buses aren't scheduled to leave for Los Angeles International Airport until 0230. Everyone is out of the barracks by 0100 and standing on the road, waiting. The excitement of finally going home has kept us all awake.

When we arrive at the airport, the morning is still dark. We board the Delta airliner and are soon in the air. Everyone on board is quiet. Perhaps, like me, they restrain themselves from being overjoyed too soon. Or they are all just tired and ready for sleep. I know the happiness of being home will overwhelm us as soon as the plane touches down in Chicago. This is when we'll realize the vision, a dream we've all shared since we departed that cold January day.

I close my eyes and let my mind wander back to the night before the land invasion. Captain Morrison told me I would be taking the first convoy into Kuwait. The fear I felt is still fresh. The dream of so many years ago about my death in a desert war had me believing I wouldn't survive.

With a small smile, I open my eyes and gaze out the window into a still-black sky.

It didn't happen. I'll soon be home.

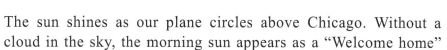

The sun shines as our plane circles above Chicago. Without a cloud in the sky, the morning sun appears as a "Welcome home" from above. Below is the city I grew up in. Lake Michigan is to our east, and Lake Shore Drive curves around the edge of the water.

On the intercom, the pilot announces, "The crew and I want to thank each of you for your service. Your country is proud of you. Welcome home."

That's followed by a few Ooh Rahs, but most Marines remain quiet. The seat belt sign comes on, and the stewardess reminds us to buckle up as the plane lines up with the runway. The familiar sight of homes and businesses reminds me of my return from Vietnam. It was at this same airport twenty years earlier. I felt lonely on that flight. No one thanked me, and no one even talked to me. This time it's different. This time we're welcomed home. We're thanked and respected for what we did over there.

Lower and lower the plane goes. Rooftops flash by. We pass the airport fence in an instant, then green grass is below us. Finally, the runway is there and then the screech of tires as the plane touches down. I'm ready to explode with joy. I didn't die. I survived my second war.

The Marines all yell "Ooh Rah" and "Hooray." The joy echoes throughout the plane. I look around, and both the first sergeant and Major Bales are laughing. The plane's crew join in our celebration.

On the ground, the plane taxis to the Air Force Reserve side of O'Hare Airport and comes to a stop. My job is the same as it was when we left here. Secure the weapons, only this time, I turn them back over to the Inspector & Instructor staff. I stand and walk toward the tail end of the aircraft while all other passengers remain seated. The same loaded .45-caliber pistol I had when we left Chicago is again on my side. The tail door opens, and I watch as the stairs are lowered to the ground. On the deck is Staff Sergeant Harden from I & I. When he sees me, he smiles a wide grin. I walk down and shake his hand.

"Welcome home, Marine," he says.

"Thanks, Staff Sergeant."

"Gunny. I'm a gunny now. Promoted March one."

I look at his collar and confirm his new rank. "Congratulations, Gunny."

"Let's get those weapons and your sidearm transferred back to our hands so you people can get the hell out of here."

"Copy that."

The weapons are off-loaded from the plane's cargo hold. I hand the gunny my sidearm, he signs the paperwork, and in less than thirty minutes, I'm back in my seat. We taxi to a regular passenger gate, where we disembark.

Still dressed in our desert cammie uniforms, I get teary eyed when I hear people cheering as we exit the plane. Some are just walking by while others are sitting down, waiting to board their flights. They clap and smile. People I don't know and will never know are cheering. As we walk to the baggage claim, we pass by folks who know us only by the uniforms we wear. It seems everyone in the airport is there to greet us. Never in all my days have I felt so appreciated.

After collecting our seabags, we exit to buses waiting to take us home. A new major I don't recognize greets Major Bales, and they both board the bus. As we pull away, everyone is talking over each other until the new major stands and gets control.

"Listen up," he yells several times until the troops quiet down. "My name is Major Hudak. I'm the commanding officer of I and I for Engineer Support Company. Welcome home. I want to give you people an idea of what's going to happen between now and when we arrive at the reserve center. Once off the expressway in Indiana, we'll have a police escort. In Gary, folks may be out on the streets to greet you. The newspapers and radio stations have all been broadcasting your arrival. There will be news reporters and television cameras present when we arrive. When you get off the bus, go to your platoon formations. Major Bales will say a few words and then dismiss you. Your families are there. They're excited to see you, as I'm sure you are to see them. However, let's maintain military discipline until you're dismissed. Don't worry about your seabags. I and I will take care of them. You can pick them up inside the commons room, where refreshments will be served."

The major looks us over. The Marines remain quiet with their eyes trained on him. "Major Bales has a few words for you."

Our major stands, and the bus erupts with Ooh Rahs. He holds up his hands to quiet everyone. "Marines, we've been part of the largest invasion force in the history of our country. We've participated in a great victory over a formidable enemy. We are better trained and better fighters. We are victors, and this is something you can be proud of. Like Major Hudak said, military discipline must remain as we exit the buses. Let's not do anything to detract from who we are and what we've accomplished." He waits a moment, and then with a smile, he cries out, "And who are we!"

"Marines!" is screamed throughout the bus, followed by more Ooh Rahs and cheering.

We leave the expressway and enter the city streets of Gary. As expected, people are cheering our return. When we finally head down Lake Street, the reserve center comes into view.

The bus pulls through the front gate and parks on the parade deck in front of a couple hundred people. They're cheering, and many of them are carrying signs that welcome us home. I look out the window, searching for Cindy and my family. There are too many faces, too many people. I can't find them. When the bus stops, we get up to exit, and I yell, "Remember what you've been told. Maintain discipline until you're dismissed. Motor T, you're on me."

Off the bus, the Marines start to form up. As the platoon commander of Motor Transport, I'm in front.

Major Bales stands before us and calls out, "Company ... At-ten-tion!" Each platoon of Marines snaps to attention. "You Marines have performed with true esprit de corps. The task you did while serving is a remarkable one, and you did it with honor." He looks from platoon to platoon, and I imagine he's proud of us. "Enjoy this time with your families. Company ... Dismissed."

As the men break formation and run to their loved ones, the family members also run to their Marines. I look into the crowd for CJ. I know she's here, I just can't find her. Then behind me I hear, "Dad." I turn around, and there's my daughter, Kimberly. We hug for a few seconds, then I pull away to look at her, saying, "I love you. I missed you."

"I love you too, Dad."

I grab her tight again, and she says, "Turn around, Dad."

With her still in my arms, I turn, and there is Cindy. Her blond hair shines, and her blue eyes sparkle. Her smile is wide. It's all I've dreamed of these last six months. I let Kimberly go and move toward CJ, who runs into my arms. We embrace and hold on, knowing how there was always the chance this day would never happen.

With tears in her eyes, she says, "I love you. I missed you so much. I have prayed for this. You're home. You're home."

I hold her close and cuddle her face in my shoulder. "I've missed you more than I can say."

She pulls away, and I look deep into her teary eyes.

"I love you more than life. You are my life." I smile, then laughing, I shout, "I love you, I love you." I pull her close again and whisper, "I love you, CJ, forever and a day." We kiss long and with passion.

Our time at the reserve center is short, and now we're ready to head out. Before I leave, I look around for a few last-minute goodbyes to some fellow Marines, like Woody and Wiśniewski. We realize words aren't important. Our smiles, hugs, and a "See ya at drill" say it all. I pick up my seabag, throw it over my shoulder, and follow the girls to the car. Cindy opens the trunk, and I toss the bag in.

As we drive out the gate, I ask, "Where are the kids?"

"They're home waiting for you. Your mom and dad and brothers are there too. A bunch of folks wanted to see you, but I said we'd have a get-together after you had some time to unwind."

"Thanks, I'll need that time."

As we enter Crown Point, I see overhead business signs reading "Welcome Home, Staff Sergeant Green." Another reads, "Job well done, Staff Sergeant Rick Green." CJ smiles as she sees I've noticed the signs. They continue all over town as business after business welcomes me back.

"How did all this happen?" I ask.

"Your daughter did that."

Kimberly explains, "I went from business to business telling them you were coming home. Explained how great it would be if they put something on their signs to welcome you. They loved the idea. In fact, as the word got out, they started calling the house, asking when to expect you. So many wanted to join in welcoming you home."

I turn to the rear seat with teary eyes and say, "Thanks, Kim. This is great."

She smiles, and now she knows how much I appreciate what she did.

When we turn down Indiana Avenue, I can see our house and the welcome-home banner hanging outside. My parents, children, and in-laws are on the driveway, ready to greet me. It's a sobering moment.

The children run to me for a giant group hug. Squeezes from my tiny mom and an embrace from my dad fill my heart. My brothers, Roy and Ben, are here with more hugs. Everything is perfect.

The day passes to night, and finally Cindy and I are alone in bed. I hold her close. At first, we don't kiss. There's no foreplay and no lust. Our naked bodies touch, and I can feel the warmth she radiates. It fills me with the love I've longed for. Vanished are the thoughts of never feeling this again. I'm overcome with emotion as I touch her.

Tears fill my eyes when I look down at her soft, beautiful face cuddled in my arm, and I know our love will never end. Our bodies come together with the desire and passion we've both only fantasized about. Our very essence fills with ecstasy. That night, we fall asleep in each other's arms. When we wake, there will be no more separation. No more farewells. We will be together, forever and a day.

The End

Before you read the Epilogue, take a minute and drop me a line. I want to know what you thought of the book. Also, if you have a little more time, go to amazon.com and leave an honest review. Those really help a self publisher. My email is greenrzilla@gmail.com My website is rickgreenbergauthor.com

Thank you for reading my book and be sure to keep an eye out for the final chapter in Greeny's life.

EPILOGUE

22 September 1993

IT'S A BEAUTIFUL SATURDAY MORNING in Kokomo, Indiana. Cindy and I arrived late last night to meet up with Roy and Coleen along with friends Jim and Peggy. Roy had invited Cindy and me to join them for this Vietnam reunion.

23 September 1993

Paramedics are breaking into Roy and Colleen's motor home. Inside they find six adults, all comatose or dead. The first medic in takes a quick pulse of a woman lying on the floor closest to the door. There's no pulse, and she's cold. "This one's dead," he yells to his partner.

He moves to the next victim lying on the dinette table turned bed. Another check for a pulse finds none. "This one's gone too."

The second medic to enter the motor home has more experience. He follows protocol and rechecks each victim. After confirming the first woman is dead, he moves to the second victim. What he discovers will shock you.

Be sure to read the continuing story, "A Marine's Faith in a Box," scheduled for release in 2019.

Made in the USA
San Bernardino, CA
29 April 2019